Geronimo St

3 IN 1

PAPERCUTZ

Geronimo Stilton

GRAPHIC NOVELS AVAILABLE FROM PAPERCUTZ

...ALSO AVAILABLE WHEREVER E-BOOKS ARE SOLD!

#1
"The Discovery
of America"

#2
"The Secret
of the Sphinx"

#3
"The Coliseum
Con"

#4
"Following the
Trail of Marco Polo"

#5
"The Great
Ice Age"

#6
"Who Stole
the Mona Lisa?"

#7
"Dinosaurs
in Action"

#8
"Play It Again,
Mozart!"

#9
"The Weird
Book Machine"

#10
"Geronimo Stilton
Saves the Olympics"

#11
"We'll Always
Have Paris"

#12
"The First Samurai"

#13
"The Fastest Train
in the West"

#14
"The First Mouse
on the Moon"

#15
"All for Stilton,
Stilton for All!"

#16
"Lights, Camera,
Stilton!"

#17
"The Mystery of the
Pirate Ship"

#18
"First to the Last Place
on Earth"

#19
"Lost in Translation"

papercutz.com

Geronimo Stilton

3 IN 1

By Geronimo Stilton

"Discovery of America"
"The Secret of the Sphinx"
"The Coliseum Con"

PAPERCUTZ
New York

GERONIMO STILTON 3 IN 1 #1
Text by Geronimo Stilton
Illustrations by Edizioni Piemme
Geronimo Stilton names, characters and related indicia are copyright, trademark, and exclusive license of Atlantyca S.p.A.
All rights reserved. The moral right of the author has been asserted.

"The Discovery of America"
Original Title: Geronimo Stilton Alla Scoperta Dell'America
Story by Geronimo Stilton
Editorial Coordination by Topatty Paciccia
Original Editing by Daniela Finistauri
Thanks to Piccolo Tao and Peperisa Peperosa
Script by Luca Crippa and Maurizio Onnis
Artistic Coordination by Gògo Gó
Artistic Assistance by Tommaso Valsecchi
Illustrations by Lorenzo De Pretto
Coloring by Davide Corsi
Graphics by Michela Battaglin
Cover Art and Color by Flavio Ferron

"The Coliseum Con"
Original title: Geronimo Stilton La Truffa Del Colosseo
Story by Geronimo Stilton
Editorial coordination by Patrizia Puricelli in collaboration with
Tommaso Valsecchi
Original editing by Daniela Finistauri
Script by Demetrio Bargellni
Artistic Coordination by Roberta Bianchi
Artistic Assistance by Tommaso Valsecchi
Graphic Project by Michela Battaglin
Graphics by Marta Lorini
Cover Art and Color by Flavio Ferron
Interior Illustrations and Color by Ambrogio M. Piazzoni

"The Secret of the Sphinx"
Original Title: Geronimo Stilton Il Segreto Della Sfinge
Story by Geronimo Stilton
Editorial coordination by Patrizia Puricelli
Original editing by Daniela Finistauri
Script by Demetrio Bargellni
Artistic Coordination by Roberta Bianchi
Artistic Assistance by Tommaso Valsecchi
Graphic Project by Michela Battaglin
Graphics by Sara Baruffaldi and Marta Lorini
Cover Art and Color by Flavio Ferron
Interior Illustrations by Gianluigi Fungo
Coloring by Mirko Babboni

© EDIZIONI PIEMME 2007-2017, S.p.A
© Atlantyca S.p.A. – via Leopardi 8, 20123 Milano, Italia – foreignrights@atlantyca.it
© 2009, 2017 for this Work in English language by Papercutz.
Based on an original idea by Elisabetta Dami
www.geronimostilton.com
Stilton is a name of a famous English cheese. It is a registered trademark of the Stilton Cheese Markers' Association.
For more information go to www.stiltoncheese.com
No part of this book may be stored, reproduced or transmitted in any form or by any means, electronic or mechanical, including,
photocopying, recording, or by any information storage and retrieval system, without written permission from the copyright holder.
For information address: Atlantyca S.p.A., via Leopardi 8, 20123 Milano, Italy
foreignrights@atlantyca.it - www.atlantyca.com

Translation – Nanette McGuinness
Lettering and Production – Manosaur Martin
Original Associate Editor – Michael Petranek
Assistant Managing Editor – Jeff Whitman
Jim Salicrup
Editor-in-Chief

ISBN: 978-1-54580-115-4
Printed in China
December 2017

Papercutz books may be purchased for business or promotional use.
For information on bulk purchases, please contact Macmillan Corporate and Premium Sales Department at (800) 221-7945 x5442.

Distributed by Macmillan
First Papercutz Printing

IT ALL STARTED ON A SCORCHING AUGUST MORNING, HERE IN NEW MOUSE CITY, THE CAPITAL OF MOUSE ISLAND. ALLOW ME TO INTRODUCE MYSELF...

THE DISCOVERY OF AMERICA

MY NAME IS STILTON, *Geronimo Stilton!* MY JOB IS TO EDIT THE RODENT'S GAZETTE, THE MOST FAMOUSE PAPER ON ALL OF MOUSE ISLAND!

WHILE MY COLLEAGUES WERE WORKING AND SWEATING AWAY, I HAD ASKED NOT TO BE *DISTURBED*; I HAD SOME IMPORTANT WORK TO GET DONE...

VERY IMPORTANT...IN FACT, ABSOLUTELY *IMPORTANT!*

SNORE SNORE

WHOOP! WHOOP!

MOLDY MOZZARELLA! THAT'S PROFESSOR VON VOLT'S ALARM!

WHOOP! WHOOP!

PROFESSOR VON VOLT! HOW NICE TO HEAR FROM YOU! HOW ARE YOU? YES, OF COURSE. I'M COMING...

...RIGHT NOW!

IN AN INSTANT, I RUSHED TO PROFESSOR VON VOLT'S LAB. MY BEST FRIEND HAD SOME *EXTRAORDINARY* NEWS...

HERE I AM! I RACED OVER!

THANKS, GERONIMO! I HAVE TO SHOW YOU SOMETHING...

THIS NEW INSTRUMENT INDICATES ANY CHANGE THAT CROPS UP IN THE PAST.

THIS DISPLAY LETS ME KNOW WHEN THE PIRATE CATS ARE TRAVELING THROUGH TIME TO CHANGE HISTORY TO BENEFIT THEM... AND THAT'S EXACTLY WHAT'S HAPPENING NOW!

THOSE PIRATE CATS! IT'S ALWAYS THEM! WHEN THEY TRAVEL TO THE PAST THEY ALSO CHANGE THE *PRESENT.* WE'VE GOT TO STOP THEM!

GERONIMO! YOU HAVE TO CALL YOUR FAMILY...

-GULP!- I REALLY THINK YOU'RE RIGHT!

IT TOOK ME NO TIME AT ALL TO TELL MY FAMILY. AND THEY'D NEVER TURN DOWN A NEW ADVENTURE! MY SISTER THEA...

I'LL POSTPONE MY TRIP TO THE AMAZON RAINFOREST!

MY NEPHEW BENJAMIN, HIS FRIEND BUGSY WUGSY...

FANTASTIC!

AND MY COUSIN, TRAP!

THE PIRATE CATS? I'M ON MY WAY!

AN HOUR LATER...

THE PIRATE CATS WENT TO 1492 IN SPAIN, THE YEAR THAT CHRISTOPHER COLUMBUS ARRIVED IN AMERICA! I'M SURE THEY WANT TO CHANGE HISTORY!

HOW WILL WE CATCH UP WITH THEM, PROFESSOR?

WITH THE SPEEDRAT, MY FRIENDS! MY LATEST INVENTION! A HIGH-TECH TIME MACHINE!

WERECAT WHISKERS!

WOW!

GRACIOUS GORGONZOLA!

PROFESSOR, YOU NEVER CEASE TO SURPRISE US!

SPEEDRAT

HOW NICE! *ANOTHER TRIP IN TIME!* BUT...HOW WILL WE KEEP THEM FROM RECOGNIZING US?

YOU'LL FIND CLOTHING AND EVERYTHING YOU NEED FOR YOUR TRIP IN THE SPEEDRAT...

VRRRR

AND HOW WILL WE BE ABLE TO UNDERSTAND EVERYONE?

WITH THIS EARPIECE! IT'S PRACTICALLY INVISIBLE AND TRANSLATES EVERY LANGUAGE!

GREAT!

AND WHAT WILL WE EAT? MY STOMACH'S ALREADY *GROWLING--* -:ACK!:-

UM, PROFESSOR, DON'T LISTEN TO HIM. TELL US WHERE THE PIRATE CATS ARE INSTEAD.

...GOOD LUCK! AND REMEMBER THAT THE *FUTURE IS IN YOUR PAWS!*

IN SPAIN, IN THE CITY OF PALOS, THE PORT THAT *COLUMBUS* SAILED FROM IN THE MONTH OF AUGUST...

NEVER FEAR, PROFESSOR! WE'LL FIND THE PIRATE CATS AND STOP THEM!

AND SO WE LEFT FOR A NEW TRIP INTO TIME! WE DIDN'T KNOW WHAT DANGERS WE WOULD FACE, BUT WE KNEW WE'D BE UP TO OUR WHISKERS IN ADVENTURE!

PALOS IS A SMALL TOWN TODAY, BUT IN THE TIME OF COLUMBUS IT WAS A LARGE PORT AND IT BECAME EVEN MORE IMPORTANT DUE TO THE DISCOVERY OF AMERICA!

Spain

Palos

BACK IN PALOS IT WAS *AUGUST 1, 1492*. THE RULERS OF SPAIN, FERDINAND AND ISABELLA, HAD ASKED CHRISTOPHER COLUMBUS TO DISCOVER A NEW ROUTE TO THE INDIES, AND THE GREAT ITALIAN NAVIGATOR WAS GETTING READY TO DEPART...

CALAMITOUS CATS! NOW WHERE WILL WE PUT THE *CATJET*?

IN THE MEANTIME, THE PIRATE CATS HAD ARRIVED IN PALOS AND WERE GETTING READY FOR THEIR MISSION...

NO ONE MUST FIND OUR *TIME MACHINE*! LET'S COVER IT UP WITH SOME OF THAT TRASH.

CATJET

HOP TO IT, HAIRBALL!

THOSE OVERFED BALLS OF FUR! I ALWAYS HAVE TO DO THE WORST JOBS!

NOW THAT WE'RE IN SPAIN, WHAT WILL WE DO? ARE WE GOING TO GO RIGHT TO THE PORT?

YEAH, *TERSILLA*! WHAT ARE WE GOING TO DO? ARE WE GOING TO GO TO SEE *REAL MADRID* PLAY?

DON'T MOUSE OFF,* BONZO! *SOCCER* HASN'T BEEN INVENTED YET!

LET'S PUT ON OUR MOUSE MASKS NOW... THEN WE CAN GET DRESSED AT THE COAST...

I HAVE TO LOOK LIKE A SAILOR, TOO!

MOUSE EARS

MOUSE NOSE

*DON'T TALK NONSENSE!

LATER, AT THE PORT...

THE PIRATE CATS WITH THEIR MOUSE MASKS ON!

LISTEN, RODENTS! I'M MINESTRONE MOUSTRONI, *THE ROYAL INSPECTOR!* I SPEAK IN THE NAME OF THE KING. WE NEED EXPERT SAILORS WHO ARE STRONG AND FEARLESS...

THE ROYAL INSPECTOR TRAVELED WITH COLUMBUS. HE WAS IN CHARGE OF REPORTING EVERY DETAIL OF THE MISSION TO KING FERDINAND AND QUEEN ISABELLA.

YOU SURE LOOK FUNNY IN THAT MOUSE MASK!

HOW DARE YOU! I'M YOUR *BOSS!*

MEOW DOWN!* DO YOU WANT THEM TO DISCOVER US!?

NEXT!

*CALM DOWN!

AND WHAT CAN YOU DO?

I'VE SERVED THREE KINGS, SAILED EVERY SEA, DISCOVERED HUNDREDS OF TREASURES AND AM AN EXPERT HELMSMAN...

SAILOR, IF HALF OF WHAT YOU SAY IS TRUE, YOU'RE JUST THE RODENT FOR US...

MY COMPANIONS AND I WOULD BE HAPPY TO SERVE UNDER THE GREAT COLUMBUS!

WHAT COMPANIONS? THOSE TWO OVER THERE?

HEY, DUMMY! YOU THINK YOU'RE A BETTER SAILOR THAN ME? WHO SAYS SO?

MY MAMA SAYS SO!

!!!

WE NEED A GOOD HELMSMAN, BUT WE DON'T WANT ANY ROUGH-NECKS. GO TELL THEM TO KNOCK IT OFF...THEN *FOLLOW ME!*

THIS IS THE **SANTA MARIA**, THE FLAGSHIP OF THE GREAT CHRISTOPHER COLUMBUS. THE OTHER TWO SHIPS ARE THE **NINA** AND THE **PINTA**.

MAGNIFICENT SHIPS, SIR! WITH THEM, WE CAN BRAVE ANY KIND OF **SEA!**

CAPTAIN! HERE ARE AN **EXPERT HELMSMAN** AND TWO **DECK HANDS** FOR YOU!

HMM... LET'S SEE WHO YOU BROUGHT ME!

MY GOOD RODENTS! DO YOU KNOW WHERE WE'RE GOING?

SURE! WE'RE GOING TO AM-- --ACK!--

NO, CAPTAIN! WE DON'T KNOW!

WE'RE SAILING TO THE **INDIES!** BUT WE'RE SAILING WEST! SO WE'RE GOING TO SHOW THAT THE EARTH IS **ROUND!**

THE INDIES, DURING THE TIME OF COLUMBUS, AMERICA'S EXISTENCE WASN'T YET KNOWN. COLUMBUS'S PLAN WAS TO KEEP SAILING WEST TO REACH THE INDIES!

CAPTAIN COLUMBUS! WE DON'T UNDER-STAND!

SUFFERING SQUEAKERS! YOU DON'T HAVE TO UNDERSTAND! YOU'RE JUST DECK HANDS!

CAN YOU TACKLE A JOURNEY THIS LONG AND **DANGEROUS?**

OF COURSE, CAPTAIN! UNDER YOUR LEADERSHIP, I'LL GUIDE THIS SHIP TO THE ENDS OF THE EARTH!

COLUMBUS SHOWS THE NEW HELMSMAN HIS SHIP...

HERE'S THE TILLER! FROM HERE YOU CAN GUIDE THE SHIP. AND IF YOU DO YOUR WORK WELL, I'LL REWARD YOU PROPERLY...

I WON'T DISAPPOINT YOU!

11

THE NEXT DAY, WE ARRIVED IN SPAIN ON THE SPEEDRAT. THOSE SCOUNDRELS WOULD GIVE US TROUBLE...

WOW! WHAT A TRIP!

PALOS IS OVER THERE!

WHO KNOWS WHERE THOSE NASTY CATS ARE HIDING...?

LET'S GO! WE HAVE TO FIND THE PIRATE CATS!

WAIT A MINUTE, UNCLE!

WHAT IS IT, BENJAMIN?

YOU DON'T WANT TO GO AROUND IN 1492 DRESSED LIKE THAT!

HOW DO I LOOK?

PROFESSOR VON VOLT'S CLOTHES FIT US PERFECTLY...

LET'S GO STRAIGHT TO THE PORT. SOMEONE SURELY WILL HAVE SEEN THOSE NASTY CATS...

PALOS WAS A CITY WITH LOTS OF SHOPS AND CRAFTSMEN AT WORK...

A SHOP THAT REPAIRS SAILS! WE'RE IN A SEASIDE CITY, FOR SURE...

CHRISTOPHER COLUMBUS DEPARTED FROM HERE ONE SUMMER MORNING...

HEY! WAIT FOR ME!!

OOPS!

SLAM

-MMPH-... GET ME OUT OF THIS SAIL!

UNCLE, TODAY IS *AUGUST 2*. DO YOU REMEMBER EXACTLY WHICH DAY COLUMBUS SAILED?

IF I REMEMBER CORRECTLY, HE SAILED ON AUGUST 3...

WE HAVE TO HURRY!

SHORTLY THEREAFTER WE ARRIVED AT THE AREA AROUND THE PORT. I WAS SURE THE CATS WOULDN'T BE TOO FAR AWAY...

OH, HOW NICE TO SAIL AWAY, ON EVERY SEA AND EVERY DAY!

WHAT CHEERFUL PEOPLE! SHALL WE GO IN AND HAVE SOMETHING TO EAT?

HEY LOOK!

WHAT DID YOU SEE?

LOOK AT THIS PILE OF TRASH...

WHAT IS IT ABOUT THIS THAT DOESN'T FIT?

BACK THEN, CITY-DWELLERS DIDN'T COLLECT THEIR TRASH; THEY THREW IT INTO THE STREET...

...BUT THEY'VE THROWN OUT SOME VERY STRANGE TRASH FROM THIS INN...

WHO COULD HAVE EATEN ALL THESE *FISH*?

WHAT A HORRIBLE SMELL!

FISH? HMM...

HEY! MOLDY MOZZARELLA!

SPLASH

WHAT ARE YOU DOING THERE?

WATCH WHAT YOU'RE DOING, YOU CLUMSY IDIOT!

EXCUSE US, BUT... WHAT KIND OF A RODENT CAN EAT SO MUCH FISH?

I THOUGHT IT WAS STRANGE THAT THOSE STRANGERS ASKED FOR FISH, TOO... USUALLY MICE LIKE CHEESE!

"I OFFERED THEM MY BEST DISHES, BUT THOSE GUYS DIDN'T WANT TO TASTE ANY OF THEM..."

NO! NO SOUP, NO CHEESE! WE WANT FISH!

YES, LOTS OF FISH! GILTHEAD, SEA BASS, AND WHITEFISH!

AND WHERE WERE THESE STRANGERS HEADED?

THEY WERE SAILORS AND WANTED TO GO TO SEA. THEY ASKED ME WHICH WAY THE PORT WAS...

THEY WERE LOOKING FOR COLUMBUS'S SHIPS... HEY! DON'T YOU WANT TO EAT SOMETHING?

COME ON! LET'S GET TO THE PORT!

-:PANT, PANT:- DO YOU KNOW WHERE COLUMBUS'S SHIPS ARE?

COLUMBUS? THAT WEIRD GUY?

TEN MINUTES LATER...

HERE'S THE PORT!

WHAT BEAUTIFUL SHIPS!

BUT HOW ARE WE GOING TO FIND THE PIRATE CATS?

OVER THERE YOU'LL FIND OTHER *FOOLS* LIKE YOU WHO WANT TO GO TO SEA WITH THAT DREAMER!

WE FINALLY GOT TO COLUMBUS'S SHIPS...

HERE THEY ARE!

COME FORWARD! THE CREW IS ALMOST COMPLETE!

THESE ARE COLUMBUS'S SAILORS! THE CATS CAN'T BE FAR OFF!

HEY! WAIT FOR ME!

OOPS!

OW!

15

MEOW!!!

LOOK WHERE YOU PUT YOUR PAWS, TAIL SMASHER!

SORRY, MISTER!

LITTLE MOUSELINGS SHOULD STAY HOME!

HE HURT YOU, EH? HA! HA!

HMM...

WHEN BENJAMIN FELL ON HIS TAIL, THAT SAILOR SAID *MEOW!*

MEOW?

NO! HE SAID CIAO!

SHUT UP! HE SAID WOW!

BUT HE SAID... BOW-WOW!

BOW-WOW? WHAT'S THAT? A NEW CURSE WORD?

I'M SURE IT WAS *MEOW!*

MEOW, EH? HMM...

THOSE TWO ARE PART OF CAPTAIN COLUMBUS'S CREW...

16

ARE YOU THINKING WHAT I'M THINKING, GERONIMO?

ALAS, YES, KID SISTER!

WHAT DO YOU THINK... OF A LITTLE OCEAN JOURNEY?

YESSSS!

HEY! JUST A MINUTE!

I DON'T KNOW ANYTHING ABOUT SAILING!

LUCKILY I'M HERE. I KNOW HOW TO DO EVERYTHING!

EVERYTHING?

GO ON, ANSWER! I'M *MINESTRONE MOUSARONI*, THE REPRESENTATIVE FOR SPAIN. AND THIS IS *MACARONI MOUSARONI*, MY WIFE!

I CAN DO MANY TRADES... I KNOW HOW TO TELL *JOKES*, DANCE, MAKE MUSIC...

AND... DO YOU KNOW HOW TO *COOK*?

YES... YES... WHY?

AND YOU, DO YOU KNOW HOW TO STYLE A LADY'S HAIR?

OF COURSE!

GOOD! WRITE IT DOWN: THIS ONE'S BOARDING! HE'LL BE THE *COOK!*

AND THIS YOUNG LADY WILL BE MY TRAVELING COMPANION...

WELL, THEN, COOK... AND TRAVELING COMPANION...

UM, I'M BOARDING, TOO...

I'M COMING, TOO!

ME, TOO!

AND WHO ARE YOU? YOU DON'T REALLY LOOK LIKE A SAILOR...

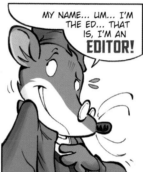

MY NAME... UM... I'M THE ED... THAT IS, I'M AN **EDITOR!**

UM, YES... I EDIT THE NEWS AND WRITE ADVENTURE STORIES...

THEN YOU CAN WRITE?

YES, AS I SAID...

GREAT! WE'VE GOT A *SCRIBE* WHO'LL WRITE THE STORY OF OUR VOYAGE!

WAP

~COFF! COFF!~

WE'D ACHIEVED OUR GOAL-- TO GET ONBOARD THE SHIPS FOR COLUMBUS'S BIG EXPEDITION...

-Cook
-Companion
-Edit

SIR, THE CREW IS COMPLETE!

WHAT CAN THEY DO?

THEY CAN WRITE! THEY'RE REGULAR *INTELLECTU-ALS!*

18

AUGUST 3, 1492, WAS A BIG DAY FOR PALOS. THE WHOLE CITY CAME TO THE PORT TO CELEBRATE COLUMBUS'S DEPARTURE...

GOODBYE, PALOS!

CIAO! WE'RE OFF!

SQUEEEAK!

BYE! BYE, EVERYONE!

I HOPE I DON'T GET SEASICK!

EVERYONE AGREES! WE'LL SHTEAL COMMAND OF THE SHIP...

BUT SOMEBODY HAD SOMETHING ELSE IN MIND...

IT'S PRONOUNCED STEAL... AND WE'LL STEAL IT WHEN I SAY SO!

HA! HA!

19

ARE WE REALLY GOING TO FIND THE INDIES, CAPTAIN?

CERTAINLY! I'VE BEEN PREPARING FOR THIS EXPEDITION FOR YEARS!

IT TOOK COLUMBUS NEARLY TEN YEARS TO FIND SPONSORS FOR HIS EXPEDITION. AS A MATTER OF FACT, HE HAD ALREADY PRESENTED HIS PROJECT IN 1483 TO THE KING OF PORTUGAL.

WE'LL FOLLOW THIS COURSE FOR TWO WEEKS. THEN, WE'LL HEAD SOUTH. THEN FINALLY WE'LL HEAD WESTWARD AGAIN. THE INDIES AREN'T FAR!

DID YOU WRITE THAT DOWN, SCRIBE? KING FERDINAND WANTS A FAITHFUL CHRONICLE OF THE TRIP.

OF COURSE! WHEN THE KING READS MY CHRONICLE, IT'LL BE AS IF HE HAD TRAVELED WITH US!

IT WILL BE A MAGNIFICENT ACHIEVEMENT!

LET'S HOPE SO!

From the scribe's chronicle.
"THE SAILORS AREN'T AFRAID OF ANYTHING..."

BRRR! THIS 'FRAIDY CAT'S SCARED!

"THE COOK NEVER STOPS WORKING, EVEN WHEN FACED WITH THE HARDEST TASKS..."

SOB! SOB! I HATE ONIONS!

"EXPERT SAILORS STEER OUR SHIPS."

WUMP

OUCH! PAY ATTENTION, YOU IDIOT!

BUT THE FOLLOWING MORNING...

CAPTAIN, WHY HAVE THE SHIPS COMPLETELY **STOPPED?**

WE'VE ENTERED AN AREA OF DEAD WATER, THAT IS, WHERE'S THERE NO WIND.

AND IF THE **WIND** DOESN'T BLOW, THE SANTA MARIA WON'T SAIL...

COME ON, COUSIN, COME PLAY WITH US!

I'M WRITING. HOW MANY TIMES DO I HAVE TO TELL YOU THAT?

COUSIN, YOU'RE A REGULAR FUSSBUDGET!

HEY!

NOW LET'S PLAY WITH YOUR DIARY... **CATCH IT!**

YES, COME ON, SCRIBE, RUN... JUMP...

GET IT FROM ME IF YOU CAN!

STOP!

HELPPP!

HEY!

SWISH

MAKE WAY!

THAT SCRIBE HAS SUCH BAD MANNERS!

STAY AWAY, SQUEAKER!

BOING

-GULP!-

OOPS... UH... OH...

GIVE IT TO ME! COME ON, I'M HERE!

SPLASH

HA! HA!

OW... OW... MY HEAD!

HEY, CALM DOWN... YOU'LL SMASH UP THE SHIP!

DOES THIS SEEM LIKE THE RIGHT TIME TO BE PLAYING AROUND?

LUCKILY THE WIND SUDDENLY CHANGED...

WE'RE MOVING! HELMSMAN, RESUME HEADING RIGHT AWAY! HEY, WHERE IS SHE?

I HAVE TO GO; COLUMBUS IS CALLING ME! BUT THINK ABOUT THIS: IF WE DON'T HAVE ANY WIND TO SAIL ON WITH NOW, WHO'S TO SAY WE'LL HAVE IT TO RETURN HOME?

HELMSMAN! WHERE ARE YOU HIDING?

WE'RE RESUMING OUR VOYAGE!

AT YOUR COMMAND, CAPTAIN!

THE WIND! THE WIND! WE'LL BE SAILING AGAIN!

OH, HOW NICE TO SAIL AWAY... ON EVERY SEA AND EVERY DAY!

A FEW DAYS LATER...

...YOU'VE GOT TO BELIEVE ME, MY TWO COUSINS, SAILORS FROM SEVILLE...

...WERE SAILING TOWARDS THE WEST, A FEW MILES OFF THE COAST OF AFRICA...

OF COURSE! I REMEMBER THEM... WHAT HAPPENED TO THEM IN THE END?

I'M NOT SURE IT'S A GOOD IDEA TO TELL YOU ABOUT IT. MY WHISKERS ARE QUIVERING WITH *FEAR*...

BE BRAVE! TELL US ABOUT IT! WE'RE NOT AFRAID OF ANYTHING!

ONE OF THEM NEVER CAME HOME AGAIN. AND DO YOU KNOW WHY? A HORRIBLE SEA **MONSTER** SPRANG UP OUT OF THE WATER...

...IT FOLLOWED THEM FOR DAYS! IT HAD TWO HEADS AND EIGHT TENTACLES WITH HOOKS AT THE ENDS, AND A MOUTH THAT SPOUTED FLAMES...

BUT IF IT FOLLOWED THEM FOR DAYS, WHY DIDN'T THEY RACE AWAY FROM IT FIRST?

AT THE START, THE ONLY SIGN IT WAS THERE WAS A TERRIBLE **STENCH**..

THE NEXT MORNING, STRANGELY ENOUGH...

WHAT A SMELL! WHAT'S GOING ON?

THAT COULDN'T BE, BY ANY CHANCE...

...THE SMELL OF THE MONSTER!

UNCLE! UNCLE! WHERE IS THAT STENCH COMING FROM? IS IT REALLY THE SMELL OF THE MONSTER?

MONSTER? WHO'S BEEN TALK-ING ABOUT *MONSTERS*? BRRR, THIS 'FRAIDY CAT'S SCARED!

THE MONSTER!

-BLECH- WHAT A STINK!

THE SMELL IS COMING FROM DOWN THERE! LET'S GO CHECK IT OUT...

BUT MAYBE...

WE HAVE TO FIND WHERE THAT SMELL COMES FROM!

IT SURE IS DARK HERE! YOU CAN'T EVEN MAKE OUT A MORSEL OF MOZZARELLA!

AND... THE STENCH IS QUITE STRONG... DO YOU WANT TO... GO ON?

HERE'S WHERE THE REPAIR SUPPLIES ARE STORED...

WHAT'S IN THESE BARRELS, UNCLE?

UM... *SAND*... TO MAKE THE SHIP STABLE...

HERE ARE THE SUPPLIES!

LET'S GET AWAY FROM HERE... WE COULD CHOKE!

WHAT A SMELL!

UNCLE! THE SMELL IS COMING FROM THIS CHEST!

WHERE? EVERYONE STOP! LET'S INFORM CAPTAIN COLUMBUS!

ON DECK, A FEW MINUTES LATER...

THUD

OPEN IT!

THE SMELL OF THE MONSTER!

THE MONSTER'S IN THE CHEST!

-UGH!-

WE SHOULDN'T HAVE OPENED IT!

-BLEH!-

-GULP!-

BLUB

MOLDY MOZZARELLA! IT'S ROTTEN FISH!

WHAAAT?!

WHO PLAYED THIS JOKE? IF I FIND THEM, I'LL MAKE THEM EAT MUSSELS FOR A MONTH...

THUD

...BETTER YET, WE'LL ABANDON THEM ON A DESERT ISLAND!

THERE'S NOTHING BETTER THAN ROTTEN FISH TO MAKE SOMEONE BELIEVE THEY'VE SMELLED A MONSTER!

A FEW HOURS HAD PASSED WHEN...

HELP!!!

HELP! HELPPP! HURRY!

WHAT'S GOING ON?

A MONSTER!

WHY ARE YOU CALLING FOR HELP?

I SAW A MONSTER!

A MONSTER! HE SAYS HE SAW A MONSTER!

THEN IT'S TRUE! WHERE THERE'S A STENCH, THERE'S A MONSTER!

WHERE DID YOU SEE IT?

IN THE SEA! IT WAS HUGE! IT HAD TWO HEADS AND EIGHT TENTACLES!

I SAW IT! I SAW IT! ME, TOO!

IT WAS ENORMOUS! IT HAD THREE HEADS AND SIX TENTACLES... NO, RATHER, IT HAD FOUR HEADS AND TWO TENTACLES...

A SEA MONSTER!

OUR LIVES ARE IN DANGER!

WE'LL BECOME CAT KIBBLE!

WHAT IS ALL THIS RACKET?

CAPTAIN, WE SPOTTED A MONSTER!

A HUGE MONSTER WITH THREE HEADS AND FIVE TENTACLES!

NO! WITH TWO HEADS AND EIGHT HOOKED TENTACLES!

SEA MONSTERS DON'T EXIST! DON'T BELIEVE THAT SUPERSTITIOUS NONSENSE!

BUT, CAPTAIN...

SILENCE! STOP WASTING TIME AND GET BACK TO WORK!

IT HAD TWO HEADS AND EIGHT TENTACLES!

NO! WE SAID THREE HEADS AND SIX TENTACLES!

TWO HEADS!

THREE HEADS!

BRAINLESS CATS!

A LITTLE LATER...

THE PAW PRINTS OF THE PIRATE CATS ARE ALL OVER THAT MONSTER STORY, I'M SURE OF IT...

YES, BIG BROTHER, IT'S TIME TO INVESTIGATE SERIOUSLY!

WHY DID I EVER LEAVE HOME? WHY? WHY? WHY?

WE BEGAN GOING AROUND ASKING QUESTIONS...

UM... IS EVERYTHING OKAY?

STEER CLEAR, SCRIBE, AND LET US PLAY IN PEACE!

SCRAM, CHEESEHEAD!

WHO DIDN'T EAT THESE CHEESE SOUFFLES?

ODD THAT THERE'S SOMEBODY ON BOARD WHO DOESN'T LIKE CHEESE...

THE SANTA MARIA'S MAST IS THE TALLEST IN THE FLEET!

UM, EXCUSE ME...

GOOD THING WE DON'T GET VERTIGO!

HEY! YOU ONLY FALL FROM HERE ONCE...

–GULP!–

LOOKIE, LOOKIE AT WHAT'S OVER HERE!

ONLY CATS CAN LEAVE THESE SCRATCHES!

WE EVEN SEARCHED AT NIGHT...

~ZZZZ... ROAR... GRUNT...~

WHAT CAN I DO ABOUT THIS?

SNORE

SNORE

FINALLY WE GOT TOGETHER TO COMPARE NOTES...

I SPENT A SLEEPLESS NIGHT, BUT I DIDN'T DISCOVER ANYTHING!

I FOUND SOME SIGNS...

I FOUND THREE PLATES OF CHEESE SOUFFLE THAT WEREN'T EATEN AND THREE CAT SCRATCHES ON THE MAST! DOESN'T THAT TELL YOU SOMETHING?

NO RODENT HAS EVER LEFT ANY OF MY CHEESE SOUFFLE!

THIS ALL CONFIRMS THAT THE CATS ARE REALLY HERE ON THE SANTA MARIA...

THOSE CATS' DAYS ARE NUMBERED...

OUCH! LOOK OUT!

ZAK

AND YOU? DID YOU FIND ANYTHING OUT? NO ONE PAYS ANY ATTENTION TO MOUSELINGS LIKE YOU...

ACTUALLY, UNCLE, WE DID NOTICE SOMETHING...

THE SAILORS WHO SCARED THE CREW WITH THOSE STORIES AND TOLD ABOUT THE STINK ARE THE SAME ONES WHO SAID THEY SAW THE MONSTER...

THIS COINCIDENCE ISN'T AN ACCIDENT... WHAT IF THEY'RE THE PIRATE CATS DRESSED AS MICE?

THEN WE SHOULD KEEP OUR EYES OPEN! BUT WATCH OUT! IT COULD BE **DANGEROUS**...

-ARGH!-

WHAP

CALAMITOUS CATS, IT'S TRUE! WE HAVE TO BE CAREFUL!

ACTUALLY, LIFE ONBOARD WAS VERY DANGEROUS...

OW!

BONK

OOPS! SORRY! HEE! HEE! HEE!

OUCH!

HA, HA, HA!

OOPS!

SPLASH

WATCH OUT, SCRIBE! WE'RE WORKING ON THE SHIP HERE!

-GLUB!- -SPIT!-

BUT WE DIDN'T YET REALIZE THAT ALL THIS WAS PART OF THE PIRATE CATS' PLAN!

YOU SHOULD HAVE SEEN THAT RODENT SPITTING! HA! HA!

HA! HA!

HEY! I'VE GOT AN IDEA! WHY NOT FIX THAT SCRIBE ONCE AND FOR ALL?

RIGHT! ONLY HE CAN PREVENT US FROM *SHTEALING* THE SHIP...

REALLY, IT'S PRONOUNCED *STEAL*... BUT LET'S THINK ABOUT THE SCRIBE LATER... REMEMBER THE PLAN: GET THE SAILORS TO MUTINY, TAKE COMMAND OF THE SHIP IN PLACE OF COLUMBUS, DISCOVER AMERICA OURSELVES AND BECOME RICH!

GOOD! SO FAR WE'VE JUST BEEN FOOLING AROUND! NOW LET'S GET SERIOUS!

A FEW DAYS LATER WE WERE HIT BY A RAGING STORM...

CREW BELOW DECKS! ONLY THE RIGGING CREW ON DECK!

WHY DID I EVER LEAVE HOME? WHY? WHY?

YOU! GET TO THE CROW'S NEST AND DON'T LOSE SIGHT OF THE NINA AND THE PINTA!

-GULP!-

BELOW DECK AND CROW'S NEST THE FIRST TERM REFERS TO THE AREA UNDER A SHIP'S DECK, UNDER COVER. THE CROW'S NEST, ON THE OTHER HAND, IS A WOODEN PLATFORM AT THE TOP OF A SHIP'S MAST.

MASTS
COLUMBUS'S SHIPS HAD THREE MASTS: IN THE CENTER WAS THE MAINMAST, IN THE PROW (THAT IS, IN THE FRONT) WAS THE FOREMAST AND IN THE STERN (THAT IS, IN THE BACK OF THE SHIP), THE MIZZENMAST.

THE MORNING AFTER THE STORM HAD FINALLY PASSED THROUGH...

DID THE STORM DO A LOT OF DAMAGE, CAPTAIN?

IT'S NO LAUGHING MATTER! BUT EVERYTHING CAN BE REPAIRED...

...EXCEPT FOR THE FORESAIL! THE SAILORS SAY IT WAS HIT BY A GUST OF WIND STRONGER THAN THE REST. BUT LUCKILY WE HAVE A SPARE...

->PSST!<- ->PSST!<- UNCLE!

WE'VE DISCOVERED SOMETHING *TERRIBLE!*

YES, UNCLE, WE DISCOVERED WHY THE SAIL BLEW AWAY! LOOK!

SEE? IT WASN'T THE WIND: THE LINE THAT HELD THE SAIL *WAS CUT, JUST LIKE THAT!*

YOU'RE RIGHT, KIDS! AND I THINK I KNOW WHO DID IT...

ARE YOU THINKING WHAT WE'RE THINKING?

YES... THIS HAS THE PAW PRINTS OF THE PIRATE CATS! BUT WHERE COULD THEY BE HIDING THEMSELVES?

33

THE JOURNEY CONTINUED PEACEFULLY FOR A FEW DAYS, UNTIL...

NOW WE HAVE THE WIND AT OUR BACKS AND WE'LL TRAVEL FASTER THAN EVER!

GOOD, CAPTAIN! I'M LOOKING FORWARD TO REACHING THE INDIES!

WE'LL HAVE A LOT TO TALK ABOUT WHEN WE RETURN!

INDEED, MY FRIENDS WILL BE SO JEALOUS!

→BLEAH!←

→GLUB!← THIS WATER IS SAAAAAAALTED!

MINE, TOO!

YUCK! SALTWATER? THAT'S IMPOSSIBLE!

CAPTAIN! WE GAVE THE SAILORS SALTWATER!

IT WOULDN'T BE ONE OF YOUR USUAL PRANKS?

I ONLY PLAY JOKES ON YOU! I DON'T KNOW WHAT COULD HAVE HAPPENED!

34

MUTINY BROKE OUT AMONG THE CREW NOW...

IT'S TRUE! WE CAN'T TAKE IT ANY MORE!

ENOUGH ALREADY! TOO MUCH HAS HAPPENED!

ROTTEN ROQUEFORT! THIS TRIP SHOULD NEVER HAVE HAPPENED!

LET'S DEMAND THAT THE CAPTAIN...

WHAT?

WHAT DO YOU WANT TO DEMAND OF THE CAPTAIN?

TO GO BACK HOME!

YES, LET'S GO HOME!

HOME! ENOUGH WITH OCEANS! LONG LIVE BATHTUBS!

RODENTS THIS VALIANT WHO WANT TO GO BACK?

THIS TRIP IS IMPOSSIBLE!

I'VE NEVER SEEN ANYTHING LIKE IT...

YES, WE'RE BEING COMMANDED BY A CHARLATAN!

STOP WASTING YOUR BREATH! WHO DOESN'T HAVE PROBLEMS AT SEA?

MANY OF YOU HAVE SAILED WITH ME BEFORE AND KNOW I ALWAYS KEEP MY PROMISES!

WE'VE ALREADY FIGURED OUT WHAT HAPPENED WITH THE WATER...

ONE OF THE BARRELS IS FULL OF SALTWATER, BUT THE OTHERS ALL HAVE THE BEST WATER THERE IS...

LISTEN TO THE COOK! IT'S A MATTER OF A SIMPLE MISTAKE WHEN WE DEPARTED. SO...

...EVERYONE GET TO WORK!

IS THAT TRUE? THAT STORY DOESN'T CONVINCE ME...

ONE MORE THING AND I'M SWIMMING BACK HOME...

MMM... WHO COULD'VE LOADED SALTWATER ONBOARD? AND WHAT ELSE CAN STILL HAPPEN?

THAT NIGHT, THE WHOLE CREW SLEPT ON THE DECK DUE TO THE HEAT...

-ZZZZ-
-ZZZZ-

-ZZZZ-

Z

I WAS DREAMING ABOUT DELICIOUS CHOCOLATE AND GORGONZOLA, WHEN..

ZZ MEOW
ZZZ
MEOW

-SNORE-
MEOW
ZZZ

MOLDY MOZZARELLA! I'LL NEVER GET TO SLEEP HERE! AND THAT SAILOR...

...SAID ...MEOW! A CAT! I'M SCARED OF CATS!

-SNORE... MEOWWW... ZZZZ... MEOWWW...-

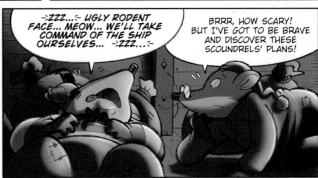

-ZZZ...- UGLY RODENT FACE... MEOW... WE'LL TAKE COMMAND OF THE SHIP OURSELVES... -ZZZ...-

BRRR, HOW SCARY! BUT I'VE GOT TO BE BRAVE AND DISCOVER THESE SCOUNDRELS' PLANS!

-ZZZZ- ... WE'LL BRING THE SHIPS TO AMERICA... -ZZZ-... WE'LL GET VERY RICH... MEOW...

!!!

MEOW... THE KING OF SPAIN WILL NAME US VICEROY... -SNORE-... ALL THE CATS IN AMERICA WILL BE ACKNOWLEDGED... -ZZZZZZ-...

THOSE COMMON CROOKS!

HOW WILL YOU DO THIS?

TOMORROW THE CREW WILL MUTINY... MEOW... AND NOW LET ME SLEEP, YOU UGLY LITTLE RAT... ⇌SNORE⇌... WE'LL DEAL WITH YOU, TOO... ⇌ZZZ⇌

MOLDY MOZZARELLA! WE'RE IN *DANGER!*

A FEW MINUTES LATER...

NOW YOU KNOW EVERYTHING I KNOW. WHAT SHOULD WE DO?

WE'LL BLOW THE WHISTLE ON THEM TO CAPTAIN COLUMBUS...

HE'LL NEVER BELIEVE OUR STORY...

LET'S WAIT UNTIL THE PIRATE CATS MAKE A WRONG MOVE...

YES, WE'LL CATCH THEM RED-PAWED!

THAT'S RIGHT, GERONIMO! WE'VE GOT TO UNMASK THEM RIGHT AS THEY SWING INTO ACTION!

HMM... ARE YOU SURE? WON'T IT BE... DANGEROUS?

LIGHTEN UP, COUSIN! I'LL HELP YOU SAVE HISTORY!

⇌*AKK!*⇌ THAT'S RIGHT! EVEN THAT MUST HAVE HAPPENED TO ME, TOO!

THE NEXT DAY, COLUMBUS THREW A PARTY...

YOU DANCE DIVINELY! AND YOU'RE AS LIGHT AS A FEATHER!

THANK YOU, SIR!

YOU DANCE LIKE A TRUE GENTLEMOUSE, SCRIBE!

YOU'RE MAKING ME BLUSH.. UM.. MA'AM...

ATTENTION! ACCORDING TO MY CALCULATIONS, WE'RE MORE THAN HALFWAY THROUGH OUR VOYAGE! TO *CELEBRATE*, THERE'S AN EXTRA RATION OF CHEESE FOR EVERYONE!

COME ON, COOK! DOUBLE RATIONS FOR EVERYONE!

I'M GOING... AND I'LL BE RIGHT BACK!

HURRAH! HURRAH!

MEALS
THE ONLY HOT MEAL OF THE DAY WAS AT 11 O'CLOCK. IN THE EVENING, COLD RATIONS OF CRACKERS AND A LITTLE DRIED MEAT AND CHEESE WERE DISTRIBUTED.

BUT IT LOOKED LIKE A HURRICANE HAD COME THROUGH THE SHIP. IN FACT, IN THE KITCHEN...

!!??

CALAMITOUS CATS! THE CHEESE IS ALL GONE? JUST YESTERDAY THERE WAS PLENTY OF IT...

THE NEWS THAT THERE WAS NO MORE CHEESE IMMEDIATELY RACED THROUGH THE SHIP...

WHAT?

→SOB!← NO GORGONZOLA APPETIZERS...

→GRUNT!← NO MOZZARELLA FOR LUNCH...

→SUPER-GRUNT!← NO GOAT CHEESE FOR AN AFTERNOON SNACK!

WHAT WILL WE DO WITHOUT CHEESE?

IF WE DON'T EAT CHEESE, WE WON'T BE BRAVE!

IF WE DON'T EAT CHEESE, WE WON'T HAVE A GOOD TRIP!

CALM DOWN! WE'VE GOT LOTS OF OTHER GOOD THINGS IN THE HOLD!

ENOUGH! ALL OF THIS FUSS FOR A PIECE OF CHEESE?

CHEESE GIVES US STRENGTH!

WE CAN'T WORK WITHOUT CHEESE!

ITS AROMA HELPS US WORK HARD!

?!? ENOUGH ALREADY! !?!

SAILORS! DO WE HAVE TO KEEP PUTTING UP WITH ALL THIS?

WHAT DO YOU MEAN, HELMSMAN?

YES, EXPLAIN!

LET'S TAKE COMMAND OF THE EXPEDITION!

WE CAN EAT ALL WE WANT AND NO ONE WILL GIVE US ANY MORE ORDERS...

BY THE FLEA-RIDDEN FUR OF A WERECAT! WHAT AN IDEA!

GO ON! WE'RE LISTENING!

THINK! HOW MANY PROBLEMS HAVE WE HAD ON THIS VOYAGE?

TAKE MY ADVICE! WE'LL GET THERE SOONER IF WE'RE IN COMMAND OF THE SANTA MARIA!

THE HELMSMAN IS RIGHT! I WANT TO EAT!

ME, TOO!

WE DON'T EVEN KNOW WHERE WE'RE GOING...

WE'RE GOING TO THE INDIES! AND I PROMISE EVERYONE WILL BECOME RICH AND FAMOUS!

DON'T BELIEVE CAPTAIN COLUMBUS! ASK HIM WHAT HE'S GOING TO DO WITH THE TREASURE FROM THE INDIES!

WE'RE SAILING UNDER THE ORDERS OF THE KING... IT'LL BE UP TO HIM TO DECIDE!

AND WHAT WILL BE LEFT FOR US? THE CRUMBS, RIGHT?

SPLASH

!!!

HEE HEE...

WATER?

BE BRAVE, COUSIN! THIS IS OUR MOMENT!

BUT... BUT...

IT REALLY IS...

..WATER!!!

MEOWWWW! I CAN'T STAND WATER!

MOUSE MASK

43

THIS CAT IS TERSILLA, THE DAUGHTER OF...

...CATARDONE, RULER OF THE PIRATE CATS!

AND THIS IS HIS ACCOMPLICE, BONZO CAT!

WE FINALLY UNMASKED THEM...

...AND WE SAVED HISTORY!

A LITTLE LATER...

I DON'T NOW HOW TO THANK YOU, SCRIBE. YOU SAVED MY MISSION!

THEY WANTED TO TAKE CONTROL OF THE SHIP BUT THEY DIDN'T SUCCEED!

NOW THAT EVERYTHING'S WORKED OUT, START THE PARTY UP AGAIN! LET'S GET DANCING!

AT YOUR ORDERS, CAPTAIN!

TAKE THESE SCOUNDRELS AWAY! WE'LL DECIDE WHAT TO DO WITH THEM LATER...

-GRRR!-

CAPTAIN COLUMBUS, I HAVE AN IDEA!

THE VOYAGE CONTINUED PEACEFULLY...

...OR JUST ABOUT!

OOPS!

MY MAP!

SPLAT

I WROTE DOWN THE STORY, TOGETHER WITH THAT MOUSE..

AND IT WAS THANKS TO ME THAT THE PIRATE CATS WERE CAPTURED...

MACARONI MOUSARONI CHOSE THE OUTFIT SHE WAS GOING TO WEAR FOR DISEMBARKING WHEN WE ARRIVED AT THE INDIES...

WHICH LOOKS BETTER ON ME, THE YELLOW OR THE RED?

BENJAMIN AND BUGSY WUGSY HAD FUN WITH THE REST OF THE CREW...

OH, HOW GOOD TO SAIL AWAY ON EVERY SEA AND EVERY DAY!

IN SHORT, EVERYONE WAS HAPPY...

I'M TELLING YOU! WE HAVE A REALLY GREAT CAPTAIN!

...WHILE THE PIRATE CATS PAID FOR THEIR MISTAKES!

IT WAS ALL YOUR FAULT!

NO! IT WAS ALL YOUR FAULT!

IT WAS ALL YOUR FAULTS!

FINALLY ONE MORNING...

OH, HOW I WISH I WERE IN NEW MOUSE CITY!

NO MORE OCEAN ADVENTURES! I'M A QUIET GUY, OR RATHER, A QUIET MOUSE...

BUT THAT... THAT IS...

LAND!

AMER--!

WHAT AM I SAYING? I MUSTN'T CHANGE THE COURSE OF HISTORY!

LAND! LAND HO! LAND HO!

WITHIN A FEW SECONDS, THE WHOLE CREW WAS CLIMBING ONTO THE DECK, ECHOING MY CRIES!

LAND!

MOLDY MOZZARELLA! I SEE IT, TOO!

IT'S REALLY LAND!

YES! IT'S LAND! I WAS RIGHT! WE REACHED THE INDIES!

AS SOON AS IT WAS DAYLIGHT, COLUMBUS DISEMBARKED...

SAN SALVADOR
COLUMBUS HAD NOT REACHED THE INDIES. THE LAND HE SAW ON OCTOBER 12, 1492, WHICH HE NAMED SAN SALVADOR, WAS AN ISLAND IN THE BAHAMAS, IN AMERICA.

I CLAIM THIS LAND ON BEHALF OF MY SOVEREIGN, THE GREAT KING OF SPAIN, FERDINAND OF CASTILE...

...AND QUEEN ISABELLA OF ARAGON...

CAPTAIN, UM...

...WE HAVE VISITORS...

!!!

WHAT'S YOUR NAME?

⚹ 📖 💬 ⚹

!?!

⚹ MY FAMILY AND I BID YOU WELCOME, STRANGER!

47

WHAT ARE YOUR PEOPLE CALLED?

OUCH!

SMACK

SORRY, UNCLE! WE WERE PLAYING!

COME ON, GERONIMO! LET'S GO PLAY, TOO!

UM, ACTUALLY... IT'S NOT NECESSARY TO SPEAK THE SAME LANGUAGE TO BE FRIENDS!

THAT EVENING, WE HAD A BIG PARTY ON THE BEACH...

HURRAH! HURRAH!

COME DANCE!

TASTE THIS, FRIEND!

HA! HA! HA!

WHAT ELSE WAS THERE TO SAY? A LONG RETURN TRIP AWAITED US...

GOODBYE! GOODBYE!

✳ BON VOYAGE!

THE SANTA MARIA CAME TO HER END ON A ROCK AND WE ABANDONED HER...

HURRY UP! EVERYONE ONBOARD THE PINTA!

MORE TERRIBLE STORMS PUT US TO THE TEST...

WHY DIDN'T I STAY IN NEW MOUSE CITY?

BEFORE REACHING SPAIN IN THE PINTA, COLUMBUS LANDED IN LISBON, WHERE HE WAS RECEIVED BY THE KING OF PORTUGAL.

WE ARRIVED IN PALOS ON MARCH 15, 1493...

GOODBYE!

IT WAS WONDERFUL TRAVELING WITH YOU!

FINALLY ON LAND...

OOPS!

SPLASH

COUSIN! WHAT ARE YOU DOING CASTING OFF AGAIN?

-»SPIT!«-
-»SPIT!«-

49

AS SOON AS THEY GOT TO LAND, THE PIRATE CATS HOTPAWED IT FROM THE SHIP AND WENT BACK HOME ON THE CATJET...

~PANT!~
~PANT!~

QUICK! LET'S MAKE TRACKS FOR THE CATJET!

MEOWWW! YOU'LL BE HEARING FROM US AGAIN...

MEANWHILE, WE TOOK THE SPEEDRAT BACK TO NEW MOUSE CITY!

FRIENDS! HOW DID IT GO?

MISSION ACCOMPLISHED! WE UNMASKED THE PIRATE CATS AND CHRISTOPHER COLUMBUS DISCOVERED AMERICA!

HURRAH! THOSE SCOUNDRELS DIDN'T CHANGE HISTORY!

BUT LET'S KEEP OUR EYES OPEN FOR THEM! I'M SURE THEY'LL TRY AGAIN!

ARE WE GOING TO TRAVEL BACK IN TIME AGAIN, PROFESSOR?

I REALLY THINK SO!

~SOB!~ I HOPE NOT! I'M A VERY QUIET GUY, OR RATHER, A VERY QUIET MOUSE!

AND NOW LET'S CELEBRATE WHAT YOU'VE DONE!

HURRAH! WE UNMASKED THE PIRATE CATS AND SAVED HISTORY!

WOW! CHEESE FOR ALL TASTES!

MY DEAR RODENT FRIENDS, FAREWELL UNTIL THE NEXT ADVENTURE... ANOTHER WHISKERFUL OF AN ADVENTURE WRITTEN BY STILTON, *Geronimo Stilton!*

IT ALL BEGAN ON A VERY COLD WINTER MORNING. NEW MOUSE CITY HAD BEEN PARALYZED BY A THREE FOOT BLANKET OF SNOW FOR DAYS...

THE SECRET OF THE SPHINX

...AND I WAS STAYING IN THE COZY WARMTH OF MY HOUSE, FULLY DRESSED, TO KEEP MY *WHISKERS FROM FREEZING!*

BUT HOW CARELESS OF ME! I'VE FORGOTTEN TO INTRODUCE MYSELF: MY NAME IS STILTON, GERONIMO STILTON! AND I EDIT THE RODENT'S GAZETTE, THE MOST FAMOUSE PAPER ON MOUSE ISLAND!

~BRRR!~

SO I WAS STAYING IN THE WARMTH WHEN THE DOORBELL RANG!

RIIING

?!?

WHO KNOWS WHO IT COULD BE IN THIS MISERABLE WEATHER...

MOLDY MOZZARELLA! I'M COMING, I'M COMING!

RIIING RIIING

WHO IS IT?

STRANGE -- I DON'T SEE ANYONE, EXCEPT FOR THIS SNOWMAN...

HMM... MAYBE I DREAMED I HEARD THE DOORBELL!

~SQUEEEAK!~

SSSS

POW

HA, HA, HA... LIKE THE TRICK, COUSIN? COME ON, LET'S HAVE A SNOWBALL FIGHT!

~SIGH~ I SHOULD'VE GUESSED... TRAP!

COME ON, OKAY? I CAN'T PLAY BY MYSELF!

YOU KNOW I DON'T LIKE SNOW VERY MUCH AND WINTER EVEN LESS!

WINTER?

~TSK~... YOU, MY DEAR GERONIMO, DON'T LIKE ANY SEASON!

"IN SPRING, THERE'S TOO MUCH **WIND**."

"IN SUMMER, IT'S TOO **HOT** AND HUMID."

"IN THE FALL, THERE ARE TOO MANY **LEAVES** ON THE GROUND."

WELL, IF YOU DON'T WANT TO PLAY... YOU CAN ALWAYS OFFER ME A CUP OF HOT CHOCOLATE!

IF THAT'S WHAT YOU WANT, JUST COME INTO THE HOUSE... ~BRRRRR!~

VROOOMM

YOO-HOO! CIAO, G! HI, TRAP!

?!?

P-PETUNIA?

SKREEE

VROOOMM

HELLO, UNCLE TRAP!

HI, KIDS! ARE YOU GOING SOMEPLACE NICE?

THE SCHOOLS ARE CLOSED, SO I'M TAKING BENJAMIN AND BUGSY FOR A RIDE ON MY NEW SNOW-MOBILE! I WANTED TO ASK G IF--

SPEAKING OF HIM, WHERE'D HE GO?

GERONIMO? HE WAS HERE JUST A MOMENT AGO!

UH-OH!

RUN INTO THE HOUSE AND LOOK FOR A SHOVEL!

I'LL HELP YOU!

OUR GERONIMO ISN'T HAPPY IF HE'S NOT IN A JAM!

INDEED! HE ALWAYS MANAGES TO GET HIMSELF INTO A FIX!

ATTENTION! ATTENTION! A MESSAGE FOR THE STILTON FAMILY!

HUH?

CALAMITOUS CATS! THAT SNOWMAN TALKS!

I REPEAT, A MESSAGE FOR THE STILTON FAMILY!

HEY! I KNOW THAT VOICE!

SQUEAK!

PROFESSOR VON VOLT! IS THAT YOU?

AH, GOOD MORNING, MISS PRETTY PAWS!

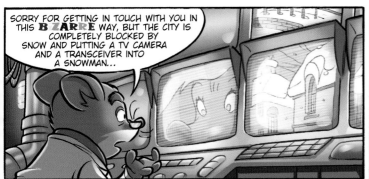

SORRY FOR GETTING IN TOUCH WITH YOU IN THIS **B ZARRE** WAY, BUT THE CITY IS COMPLETELY BLOCKED BY SNOW AND PUTTING A TV CAMERA AND A TRANSCEIVER INTO A SNOWMAN...

...SEEMED LIKE THE EASIEST WAY TO CONTACT GERONIMO!

YOU'RE REALLY A **GENIUS**, PROFESSOR!

THANKS! I NEED TO SEE GERONIMO AND YOU ALL URGENTLY!

WHERE ARE YOU, PROFESSOR?

I'LL GIVE YOU THE DIRECTIONS TO MY SECRET LABORATORY RIGHT NOW! BUT I DON'T SEE GERONIMO: WHERE IS HE?

UM, AT THE MOMENT HE'S... OCCUPIED!

ONCE AT PROFESSOR VON VOLT'S LAB...

WE'RE HERE, PROFESSOR!

SORRY FOR THE DELAY, BUT WE RAN INTO SOME **DIFFICULTIES!**

!?

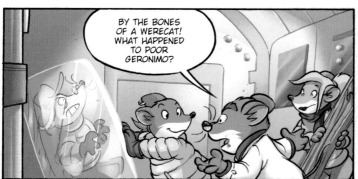

BY THE BONES OF A WERECAT! WHAT HAPPENED TO POOR GERONIMO?

IT'S A LONG STORY! ANYHOW, WE JUST NEED TO WARM HIM UP A BIT...

IN THAT CASE, I'VE GOT SOMETHING THAT WILL DO THE TRICK... A SOLAR *ENERGY LAMP* FOR MELTING METAL!

OH, THAT'S PERFECT, PROFESSOR!

SWIIISH

HANG IN THERE, COUSIN! YOU'LL BE FREE IN A FEW MINUTES...

BZZZ

WHY DID YOU WANT TO SEE US, PROFESSOR?

HUH?

AH, YES... IT'S BECAUSE OF THE TEMPOGRAPH, THE INSTRUMENT I INVENTED TO KEEP AN EYE ON THE PAST! EVER SINCE THIS MORNING, THE DISPLAY HAS BEEN INDICATING A CHANGE... SOMEONE IS TRYING TO CHANGE HISTORY!

OH, NO! THAT MEANS THE PIRATE CATS ARE BACK IN ACTION, RIGHT?

THOSE NASTY CATS!

EXACTLY! THEY'RE TIME-TRAVELING AGAIN AND, KNOWING THEM, THEIR JOURNEY CAN ONLY HAVE ONE GOAL...

...CHANGING HISTORY TO BENEFIT THEM!

THEN WE HAVE TO LEAVE IMMEDIATELY!

WHERE ARE THE PIRATE CATS HEADED?

TO MEMPHIS, THE CAPITOL OF *ANCIENT EGYPT*, IN THE YEAR 2484 B.C., DURING THE REIGN OF THE FOURTH DYNASTY PHARAOH, CHEPHREN!

DO YOU HAVE ANY IDEA WHY THE CATS CHOSE THIS TIME PERIOD?

ONLY SOME SUSPICIONS, MISS PRETTY PAWS!

CHEPHREN BUILT A LARGE PYRAMID. BUT MORE THAN THAT, ACCORDING TO SOME SCHOLARS HE ALSO FINISHED ONE OF THE MOST FAMOUS MONUMENTS IN HISTORY: THE SPHINX!

THE SPHINX
HAS THE BODY OF A LION AND THE HEAD OF A MAN. ACCORDING TO SOME SCHOLARS, ITS FACE REPRESENTED THAT OF THE PHARAOH CHEPHREN. 187 FEET LONG AND 65.7 FEET HIGH, IT'S CARVED FROM A SINGLE STONE, AND WAS ORIGINALLY PAINTED IN COLOR.

WHATEVER THE CATS' GOAL MAY BE, WE'LL ONLY DISCOVER IT BY GOING THERE. HURRY UP, GUYS. LET'S GO!

HURRAY! ANOTHER JOURNEY INTO HISTORY!

WELCOME BACK, GERONIMO!

YEOOWWW! IT'S BURNING! IT'S BURNING!

?!!

WAIT, I'LL HELP YOU PUT OUT YOUR TAIL!

→EEEPP!←

STOMP

BENJAMIN? PROFESSOR VON VOLT?

UNCLE GERONIMO!

GERONIMO, ARE YOU ALL RIGHT?

I'M FINE! BUT WHAT AM I DOING IN PROFESSOR VON VOLT'S LAB?

THERE'S NO TIME TO EXPLAIN! I'LL TELL YOU EVERYTHING ON THE WAY!

ON THE WAY? WHAT WAY? I CAN'T LEAVE, I HAVE A NEWSPAPER TO RUN!

MOLDY MOZZARELLA! I CAN'T LEEEAVE!

GET MOVINGGGG!

?

UM... DON'T FORGET MY SPECIAL EARPIECES THAT LET YOU SPEAK AND UNDERSTAND THE LANGUAGE FROM THAT TIME!

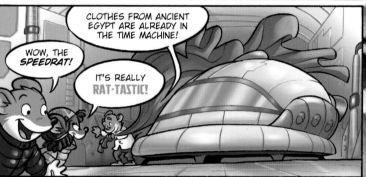

CLOTHES FROM ANCIENT EGYPT ARE ALREADY IN THE TIME MACHINE!

WOW, THE SPEEDRAT!

IT'S REALLY RAT-TASTIC!

BE SURE TO TAKE CARE OF THIS SITUATION, BECAUSE IF THE PIRATE CATS ALTER THE PAST, THEY'LL ALSO CHANGE THE PRESENT -- AND THAT MUST NEVER HAPPEN!

DON'T WORRY, PROFESSOR, WE'LL STOP THE PIRATE CATS! ⸱÷ SOB⸳÷ GOODBYE, PROFESSOR...

÷ SOB⸳÷ GOODBYE, PROFESSOR...

FASTEN YOUR SEAT BELTS!

WAIT A MINUTE, PETUNIA... I'VE CHANGED MY MIND... IT'S BETTER IF I STAY HOME...

ZZIIIP

FROOM

GOOD LUCK, MY FRIENDS!

ZZZAAP

THAT'S THE WAY WE WERE CATAPULTED INTO THE PAST... DESTINATION: ANCIENT EGYPT!

MEANWHILE, AT THE GATES OF MEMPHIS, IN ANCIENT EGYPT...

HURRY UP AND COVER THE SHIP WITH SAND, BONZO!

EGYPTIAN CIVILIZATION
IN 3000 BC, THE LEGENDARY KING, MENES, UNIFIED ALL THE TRIBES THAT HAD UP TO THEN LIVED SEPARATELY FROM EACH OTHER ALONG THE BANKS OF THE NILE RIVER AND SO BEGAN THE FIRST OF THE THIRTY DYNASTIES OF PHARAOHS. FROM THEN ON, EGYPTIAN CIVILIZATION DEVELOPED UNTIL IT REACHED A VERY HIGH LEVEL OF KNOWLEDGE: IT WAS REALLY THE EGYPTIANS WHO CREATED ONE OF THE FIRST FORMS OF WRITING. IN ADDITION, THEY DEVOTED THEMSELVES TO POETRY, SCULPTURE, ARCHITECTURE, MATHEMATICS AND MEDICINE.

MEMPHIS
FOUNDED AROUND THE END OF THE FOURTH MILLENNIUM BC, THE CITY OF MEMPHIS WAS THE CAPITAL OF EGYPT DURING THE PREDYNASTIC PERIOD (2920-2575 BC) AND THE OLD KINGDOM (2575-2134 BC).

GIZA

MEMPHIS

NILE RIVER

I'M CATARDONE, RULER OF THE PIRATE CATS. I CAN'T GET MY PAWS DIRTY!

⁓ *PUFF! PANT!* ⁓ SO I HAVE TO DO EVERYTHING BY MYSELF?

CERTAINLY! AS THE LEADER, CATARDONE'S JOB IS... TO THINK!

OF COURSE!

-: GULP! :-
TO THINK? WHAT ABOUT, TERSILLA?

HOW TO REACH OUR GOAL, NATURALLY!

HA, HA, HA... OF COURSE!

SCRITCH SCRITCH

HMMM...

BONZO, LET'S HEAR IF YOU REMEMBER OUR GOAL!

UMM... COVERING THE TIME MACHINE WITH SAND?

THE SPHINX, YOU IDIOT... THE SPHINX! WE'RE GOING TO CONVINCE PHARAOH TO GIVE IT THE FACE OF A CAT! THAT WAY WE'LL BE REMEMBERED FOREVER!

AND HOW WILL WE MANAGE TO CONVINCE PHARAOH TO DO THAT?

WE'LL USE OUR TYPICAL CAT SHREWDNESS!

YES, I'M SHREWD, VERY SHREWD, VERY, VERY SHREWD!

MEOW... I WASN'T TALKING ABOUT YOU, BONZO!

COME ON! LET'S PUT ON OUR MOUSE MASKS. THEN YOU CAN DRESS UP AS PRIESTS OF THE GODDESS BASTET, THE PATRON GODDESS OF CATS... I'LL BE A TEMPLE DANCER!

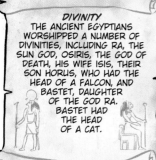

DIVINITY
THE ANCIENT EGYPTIANS WORSHIPPED A NUMBER OF DIVINITIES, INCLUDING RA, THE SUN GOD, OSIRIS, THE GOD OF DEATH, HIS WIFE ISIS, THEIR SON HORUS, WHO HAD THE HEAD OF A FALCON, AND BASTET, DAUGHTER OF THE GOD RA. BASTET HAD THE HEAD OF A CAT.

-: NNNGGG! :-

HMPH! MY MASK MUST HAVE SHRUNK OVER THE PAST FEW MONTHS!

NO, DADDY DEAR, YOU'VE PUT ON WEIGHT!

THERE, I'M DONE! NO ONE WILL SUSPECT THAT THE **CATJET** IS HIDDEN UNDER THIS SAND MASTERPIECE!

?!

DO YOU WANT TO LET EVERYONE KNOW THAT WE COME FROM THE FUTURE?!? SKYSCRAPERS DON'T EXIST YET HERE!

NO, I...

DESTROY THIS MOUSURDITY!*

~SOB!~

*ABSURDITY

SO, HALF AN HOUR LATER...

NOW THAT THE CATJET IS WELL HIDDEN AND WE ARE DRESSED LIKE MICE FROM ANCIENT EGYPT, LET'S SWING INTO ACTION!

YES, TERSILLA!

Y-Y-YES, TERSILLA!

HOW COME YOUR DAUGHTER GIVES THE COMMANDS, IF YOU'RE THE BOSS?

HUH?

TERSILLA DOESN'T GIVE COMMANDS! SHE RESTRICTS HERSELF TO JUST EXPRESSING MY THOUGHTS!

~SIGH!~ WHY DO I HAVE TO PUT UP WITH **DUMMIES** LIKE THESE TWO?!?

A LITTLE LATER, AT THE ROYAL PALACE IN MEMPHIS...

NOBLE VIZIER RAT-KARLIE, TWO PRIESTS OF THE GODDESS BASTET ARE REQUESTING AN AUDIENCE!

THE VIZIER
WAS THE PHARAOH'S PRIME MINISTER AND WORKED WITH THE PHARAOH IN DIRECTING NUMEROUS AFFAIRS OF STATE. HE WAS, THEREFORE, IN CHARGE OF CONVEYING THE ORDERS OF THE KING, COLLECTING TAXES, ADMINISTERING JUSTICE, CHECKING ON THE PROGRESS OF PUBLIC PROJECTS AND THE FLOW OF TRANSPORTATION ON THE RIVER.

PRIESTS?
ALL RIGHT, SEND THEM IN!

YES, MY LORD!

WHATEVER THE REASON FOR THEIR VISIT, IT'S BETTER TO TREAT THEM WITH RESPECT AND NOT ANNOY THE GODS.

PRIESTS
IN ANCIENT EGYPT, PRIESTS CELEBRATED THE RELIGIOUS RITES FOR WORSHIPPING THE DIFFERENT DIVINITIES. AS A RESULT, THERE WERE MANY TO KEEP UP WITH AND THEY ENJOYED NUMEROUS PRIVILEGES.

THANK YOU FOR RECEIVING US, OH MOST ILLUSTRIOUS VIZIER! I AM CAT-SINUHE AND THIS IS BON-ZETET. WE ARE PRIESTS OF THE GODDESS BASTET.

I, ON THE OTHER HAND, AM RAT-SHEPSUT, TEMPLE DANCER FOR THE GODDESS BASTET.

TELL ME EVERYTHING! UNFORTUNATELY I CAN ONLY GIVE YOU A LITTLE TIME!

→YAWN!←

THAT WILL BE ENOUGH TIME TO SHOW YOU THE MOST INCREDIBLE **MiRACLE!**

BON-ZETET HAS RECEIVED A GIFT FROM THE GODDESS BASTET.

AND THAT IS? NOT THE APPEARANCE OF INTELLIGENCE, IT SEEMS TO ME!

~ZZ~

ONE NIGHT, BON-ZETET FELL ASLEEP NEXT TO A STATUE OF THE GODDESS BASTET, AND EVER SINCE THEN, WE'VE DISCOVERED THAT THE GODDESS SPEAKS THROUGH HIM...

ALL YOU HAVE TO DO IS STEP ON HIS TAIL... LIKE THIS!

MEOOOWWW!

STOMP

M-M-MEOW?!?

THAT WAS THE WAIL OF A CAT... EVEN THOUGH HE'S A MOUSE, LIKE US!

IT'S THE GODDESS BASTET WHO'S SPEAKING!

HMM... HOW CAN I BE SURE THIS ISN'T SOME KIND OF *TRICK*?

IF YOU DON'T BELIEVE US, MOST ILLUSTRIOUS VIZIER, TRY IT YOURSELF!

YES, MOST ILLUSTRIOUS VIZIER, JUST TREAD ON HIS TAIL!

HEY... JUST A MINUTE!

HMM... THE GODDESS BASTET... WHO SPEAKS...

UH-OH!

NAAAH! IT'S NOT POSSIBLE!

~PHEWWWW!~

!

YANK

63

MEOOOWWWW!

NOW ARE YOU CONVINCED OF THE MIRACLE, MOST ILLUSTRI-OUS RAT-KARLE?

YES. ACTUALLY, I'M CURIOUS TO KNOW WHAT HE'S SAYING!

IT'S BETTER THAT WE DON'T! BUT IF YOU TAKE US IN YOUR SERVICE, OUR DANCER WILL TRANSLATE THE MESSAGES OF THE GODDESS!

AS A MATTER OF FACT, SHE ALONE CAN UNDERSTAND THE WORDS OF THE GODDESS!

REALLY? AND HAS THE GODDESS EVER SPOKEN ABOUT ME?

BUT OF COURSE, *MOST ILLUSTRIOUS VIZIER!* IT WAS ACTUALLY THE GODDESS BASTET WHO ORDERED US TO COME HERE!

SHE SAID, "GO TO MEMPHIS AND TAKE MY ADVISERS TO RAT-KARLE, VIZIER TO CHEPHREN, A RODENT WHOSE INTELLIGENCE IS GREATER THAN ANYONE ELSE'S!"

EVEN PHARAOH'S?

PHARAOH'S AND THE WHOLE ROYAL FAMILY.

THE GODDESS GAVE YOU A **SPECIAL** GIFT, TOO?

YES, OF COURSE... INTELLIGENCE!

STRANGE... I HADN'T NOTICED THAT!

→GULP!←

OKAY, I'LL TAKE YOU INTO MY SERVICE! YOUR ARRIVAL AND THE FAVOR OF BASTET WILL BE A BLESSING FOR ALL OF EGYPT!

YOU WON'T REGRET IT, OH MOST ILLUSTRI-OUS VIZIER!

→SOB!← I PREDICT HARD TIMES FOR MY TAIL!

MORE INTELLIGENT THAN PHARAOH CHEPHREN AND THE ROYAL FAMILY! THE GODS HAVE BIG PLANS FOR ME...

WE FINALLY ARRIVED IN **Egypt**...

-¿SQUEEAK!¿-

CLANG

OOPS... SORRY ABOUT THE LANDING!

-¿GROAN¿-... I THINK MY *TAIL'S* BRUISED!

HEY! WHERE DID WE END UP?

THE SHIP COMPUTER SAYS WE ARE 11 MILES NORTH OF MEMPHIS!

MOLDY MOZZARELLA! WE LANDED IN THE DESERT!

IT'S LIKELY THERE'S AN ERROR IN THE SHIP COMPUTER FROM WHEN TRAP SUBSTITUTED FOR ME AS DRIVER!

HEY, WHAT'S IT GOT TO DO WITH ME?

YOU'RE THE ONE WHO REPRO-GRAMMED THE COMPUTER BECAUSE YOU WANTED TO STOP OFF IN THE MIDDLE AGES... FOR A SNACK!

→TSK←... MAYBE IT HAPPENED WHEN YOU HOPPED AROUND ALL OVER THE PLACE JUST BECAUSE I TICKLED YOU!

IT'S NOT MY FAULT I'M TICKLISH!

THE FACT REMAINS THAT WE NOW FIND OURSELVES IN A DESERT MORE DESERTED THAN THE SAHARA!

!

WELL, MAYBE IT'S NOT QUITE THAT DESERTED! LOOK!

ROTTEN ROQUEFORT! A PYRAMID!

IT'S GIGANTIC!

OF COURSE, WE LANDED ON THE GIZA PLATEAU! THIS HAS TO BE THE PYRAMID OF CHEOPS!

GIZA PLATEAU
NORTH OF MEMPHIS, IT WAS CHOSEN BY THE PHARAOH CHEOPS, CHEPHREN'S FATHER, AS THE SITE FOR HIS OWN PYRAMID. AT 480 FEET IN HEIGHT AND 656 FEET ALONG EACH SIDE AT THE BASE, THE PYRAMID OF CHEOPS IS THE LARGEST PYRAMID IN ANCIENT EGYPT. IT TOOK OVER 20 YEARS TO BUILD AND MORE THAN 2,000,000 BLOCKS OF STONE THAT WEIGHED AROUND 2.5 TONS EACH. THE PYRAMIDS OF CHEPHREN, HIS SON MICERINO, AND THE SPHINX WERE ALSO BUILT AT GIZA.

COME ON! LET'S HIDE THE TIME MACHINE AND GET OURSELVES READY!

AFTER PUTTING ON CLOTHING FROM THAT TIME PERIOD...

DONE! THE SPEEDRAT WON'T ATTRACT ANY PRYING EYES UNDER THIS DUNE!

UNLIKE MY KILT! I FEEL RIDICULOUS, PETUNIA!

GERONIMO YOU'RE **ALWAYS** RIDICULOUS, DON'T YOU KNOW THAT? EVEN WHEN YOU'RE WEARING NORMAL CLOTHES!

THANK YOU, TRAP!

I HOPE WE MEET SOMEONE WE CAN ASK FOR DIRECTIONS. OTHERWISE WE MAY GET LOST!

IT'S SO HOT! I ALMOST MISS THE COLD OF NEW MOUSE CITY!

TELL ME ABOUT IT, BENJAMIN!

HEY! THERE'S A CONSTRUCTION SITE OVER THERE! THEY'RE BUILDING ANOTHER **PYRAMID!**

IT DEFINITELY HAS TO BE CHEPHREN'S. HE'S THE PHARAOH WHO RULED IN THIS ERA!

DID YOU NOTICE, UNCLE G? TO THE RIGHT OF THE PYRAMID IS ANOTHER MONUMENT... BUT IT'S ALL COVERED UP...

THAT HAS TO BE THE SPHINX, WHICH HASN'T BEEN FINISHED YET!

LET'S TURN ON THE EARPIECES PROFESSOR VON VOLT GAVE US AND GET CLOSER!

CLICK

SO WE WENT CLOSER TO THE PYRAMID CONSTRUCTION SITE...

CHIN UP, ONE MORE PUSH! IT'S THE LAST STONE **OF THE DAY!**

-NNNNGGG!-

HELLO! CAN YOU SHOW US THE WAY TO GET TO MEMPHIS?

!?

AND WHO ARE YOU? I'VE NEVER SEEN YOU AT THE SITE BEFORE!

WE'RE VISITORS FROM FAR AWAY! MY NAME IS *ST...GERON-ANKH-AMON!* I'M A SCRIBE!

SCRIBES
IN ANCIENT EGYPT, SCRIBES WERE AMONG THE FEW WHO KNEW HOW TO WRITE. THEY WROTE ON SHEETS OF PAPYRUS, USING PEN NIBS MADE FROM REED OR CANE THAT WERE FIRST SOAKED IN WATER AND THEN DIPPED IN INK.

MY NAME IS RATTY-ATUM AND I'M THE CHIEF ARCHITECT OF THE DIVINE PHARAOH CHEPHREN!

-NNNNNGG!-

I'M IN CHARGE OF THE WORK ON HIS PYRAMID!

SNAP

RRUUUMBLE

~SQUEEEAK!~

THESE ARE MY FRIENDS PET-NEFRET, MY COUSIN RAT-TRAP, MY NEPHEW BEN-JA-PET AND HIS FRIEND BUG-SI-WUG...

WATCH OUT! THE STONE, THE STONE!

RRUUUMBLE

BY THE EYES OF RA!

FLEA-BITTEN WERECAT FUR!

ZOOM

QUICK, MOVE AWAY!

SLAM

WHAT WAS THAT?

I-I-I'M OKAY!

ARE YOU ALL RIGHT, KIDS?

YES, BUT--WAIT A MINUTE! WHERE IS UNCLE GERON-ANKH-AMON?

ON THE OTHER HAND, THE KIDS BARELY TOUCHED THEIR DINNER!

POOR LITTLE MOUSELINGS, THEY WERE SO TIRED THAT THEY FELL RIGHT ASLEEP!

~ZZZ~

SO TELL ME, FRIEND, WHAT BRINGS YOU TO MEMPHIS?

WELL, NOW...

WE'RE HERE TO VISIT THE *capitol!*

UMM... EXACTLY!

WHAT A SPLENDID IDEA!

IF YOU'LL PERMIT ME, I'LL BE YOUR GUIDE... I COULD TAKE YOU TO VISIT THE ROYAL PALACE!

THE ROYAL PALACE?

OF COURSE! THE PHARAOH WILL BE HAPPY TO MEET THE RODENTS WHO SAVED MY LIFE!

YOU'RE VERY KIND, RATTY-ATUM, BUT WE DON'T WANT TO BOTHER YOU!

THEY SAY THE COURT OF CHEPHREN IS LUXURIOUS IS IT?

IT'S AT LEAST A BIT PHARAOH-NICAL ...AND EVER SINCE THE TWO PRIESTS AND DANCER OF THE GODDESS BASTET ARRIVED...

...IT'S GOTTEN MORE *LUXURIOUS!*

???

VIZIER RAT-KARUE DOES EVERYTHING THOSE PRIESTS ORDER AND DRAWS FROM THE ROYAL COFFERS TO SATISFY THEIR EVERY REQUEST!

"THEY ASKED FOR SOLID GOLD STATUES OF CATS AND THE GODDESS BASTET..

...AND OFFERED THE GODDESS BASTET FRESH FISH DELIVERED DAILY FROM THE COAST..."

WHAT'S MORE, THEY EVEN WANTED TO DEDICATE THAT GIGANTIC MONUMENT NEAR CHEPHREN'S PYRAMID TO THE GODDESS!

THE ONE THAT HAS THE BODY OF AN ANIMAL BUT NO FACE CARVED YET?

THAT'S THE SPHINX!

EXACTLY! ACCORDING TO THE PRIESTS, IT SHOULD HAVE THE HEAD OF A CAT RATHER THAN PHARAOH'S FACE!

WHAAAAAAT?

HORRIFYING, DON'T YOU THINK?

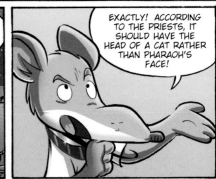

HMM... THE HEAD OF A CAT... I SMELL THE *STINK* OF THE PIRATE CATS!

RIGHT, IT CAN'T BE A COINCIDENCE!

BUT I DIDN'T SEE ANY WORK BEING DONE ON THE NEW MONUMENT!

NO, ACTUALLY, WORK HAS STOPPED...

THERE'S BEEN A *DISPUTE* BETWEEN THE PHARAOH AND THE VIZIER! THE PROBLEM IS REALLY ABOUT FINISHING THE FACE...

"ONE DAY, I SAT IN ON ONE OF THEIR DISCUSSIONS ABOUT IT..."

I DEMAND THAT THE MONUMENT WITH THE BODY OF A LION SACRED TO US HAVE MY FACE!

ANIMALS
IN THE ANCIENT EGYPTIAN RELIGION, SOME ANIMALS WERE CONSIDERED SACRED, INCLUDING CATS, CROCODILES, FALCONS, SNAKES, LIONS, AND JACKALS. SCRIBES ALSO USED THE IMAGES OF ANIMALS AS SIGNS FOR WRITING.

BUT, DIVINE PHARAOH, IT'S BASTET WHO HAS ASKED THAT IT HAVE THE FACE OF A CAT. IF WE DON'T CARRY OUT HER COMMANDS, THE GODDESS MAY AVENGE HERSELF ON US!

I'M THE SON OF THE SUN! I'M ALSO A GOD! THE GODDESS BASTET WILL UNDERSTAND MY REASONS!

PHARAOH
ANCIENT EGYPTIANS BELIEVED THAT THE PHARAOH WAS THE HUMAN INCARNATION OF THE GOD HORUS, A GOD WITH THE HEAD OF A FALCON AND THE SON OF THE SUN GOD.

WHICH THE VIZIER DIDN'T DARE ANSWER BACK TO! ANYHOW, FOR THE MOMENT, THE PROJECT IS BLOCKED!

THANK GOODNESS!

OH, BUT I'VE BEEN BORING YOU WITH ALL MY CHATTERING! I'LL BET YOU'RE ALL WORN OUT FROM YOUR JOURNEY!

AS A MATTER OF FACT, IT FEELS LIKE THE JOURNEY TOOK CENTURIES!

MORE THAN CENTURIES... *MILLENNIA!*

YOU'D DO WELL TO FOLLOW THE EXAMPLE OF YOUR FRIENDS AND GET SOME REST! WE HAVE A BIG DAY AHEAD OF US TOMORROW!

SNORE SNORE

SNORE, SNORE!

SNORE

73

74

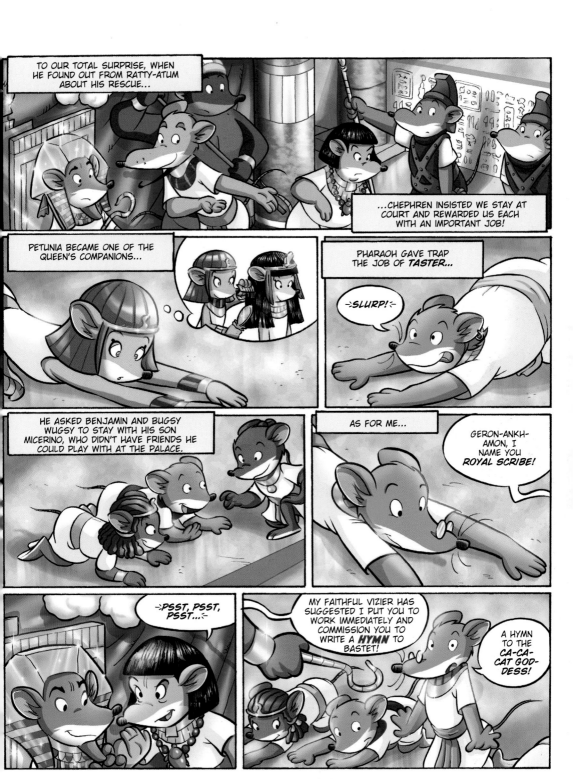

TO OUR TOTAL SURPRISE, WHEN HE FOUND OUT FROM RATTY-ATUM ABOUT HIS RESCUE...

...CHEPHREN INSISTED WE STAY AT COURT AND REWARDED US EACH WITH AN IMPORTANT JOB!

PETUNIA BECAME ONE OF THE QUEEN'S COMPANIONS...

PHARAOH GAVE TRAP THE JOB OF *TASTER*...

⁓SLURP!⁓

HE ASKED BENJAMIN AND BUGSY WUGSY TO STAY WITH HIS SON MICERINO, WHO DIDN'T HAVE FRIENDS HE COULD PLAY WITH AT THE PALACE.

AS FOR ME...

GERON-ANKH-AMON, I NAME YOU *ROYAL SCRIBE!*

⁓PSST, PSST, PSST...⁓

MY FAITHFUL VIZIER HAS SUGGESTED I PUT YOU TO WORK IMMEDIATELY AND COMMISSION YOU TO WRITE A *HYMN* TO BASTET!

A HYMN TO THE CA-CA-CAT GOD-DESS!

SPEAKING OF BASTET, WHERE ARE THE PRIESTS?

I'LL HAVE THEM SUMMONED, OH, DIVINE ONE!

A LITTLE LATER...

HIS EXCELLENCIES CATSINUHE AND BONZETET, AND THE DANCER RATSHEPSUT!

I WOULD LIKE TO INTRODUCE YOU TO MY NEW GUESTS!

?!

~GULP!~ GERONIMO STILTON AND HIS FRIENDS?

~GULP!~ THAT'S GE-GE-GE...

!

MEOOOWWW!

BAM

MEOW?!?

BOW DOWN! THE GREAT GODDESS BASTET HAS SPOKEN!

DON'T KEEP US GUESSING, RAT-SHEPSUT... ONLY YOU CAN TRANSLATE THE WORDS OF THE GODDESS BASTET!

?!?

AS ALWAYS, BASTET WISHES THE PHARAOH A LONG LIFE! IN ADDITION, SHE SENDS A WARM GREETING TO HIS NEW FRIENDS!

EXCELLENT! THANK HER FOR HER **PRECIOUS WORDS!**

GERON-ANKH-AMON, I WANT THE HYMN FOR THE GODDESS BASTET TO BE READY BY NEXT WEEK, FOR THE FESTIVAL IN HONOR OF MY ANNUAL VOYAGE DOWN THE NILE RIVER!

UMM, AT YOUR ORDERS, DIVINE PHARAOH!

GOOD, NOW MY SERVANTS WILL SEE YOU AND YOUR FRIENDS TO YOUR ROOMS!

WE THANKED RATTY-ATUM, PROMISING TO SEE HIM AGAIN SOON, AND THEN WENT TO OUR ROOMS.

PETUNIA AND I TOLD EVERYONE WHAT WE'D REALIZED ABOUT THE SPHINX AND ITS CONSTRUCTION, AND THEN WE GOT TO THE HEART OF THE MATTER.

THE "MEOW" OF THAT PRIEST WAS HIGHLY SUSPICIOUS... AND NOT THE GODDESS BASTET! IN MY OPINION, THAT WAS REALLY A CAT!

78

MEOW DOWN*, DADDY DEAR! KEEP AN EYE ON THEM AND TRY TO THINK OF A WAY TO GET RID OF THEM WITHOUT ANYONE SUSPECTING US!

*CALM DOWN

OKAY! IN THE MEANTIME, WHAT ARE YOU GOING TO DO?

I'M GOING TO CONCENTRATE ON RAT-KARLIE: BY HOOK OR BY CROOK, THE SPHINX WILL HAVE THE FACE OF A FELINE!

THE FOLLOWING DAY, WE FOCUSED ON OUR TASKS, AND THERE WAS LITTLE TIME LEFT OVER FOR US TO INVESTIGATE...

WOE IS ME! I'M A JOURNALIST, NOT A WEAVER!

TESSITURA
THE CLOTHES WORN IN ANCIENT EGYPT WERE MOSTLY MADE OUT OF VERY FINE LINEN, ALMOST VOILE. THE FABRIC WAS MADE FROM THE FIBERS AND STEMS OF THE LINEN PLANT, WHICH WAS THEN TWISTED INTO YARN AND WOVEN ON A WOODEN LOOM.

YIKES! YOU'VE NIBBLED ON EVERYTHING! HOW CAN I SERVE IT TO THE PHARAOH?

YUM, YUM... THIS IS GOOD, TOO.

HEE, HEE, HEE!

IT'S SO NICE TO PLAY TOGETHER!

HA, HA, HA!

→BRRR←...JUST LOOKING AT THIS GODDESS BRINGS UP MY SCAREDY-CAT FRIGHT!

IT'LL BE HARD TO PUT A LONG HYMN ON A SINGLE PAPYRUS! EVEN MORE SO WITH HIEROGLYPHICS -- I DRAW VERY BADLY!

PAPYRUS IS A PLANT WITH A LONG STEM AND LEAVES THAT GROWS IN THE SWAMPS ALONG THE NILE RIVER. IT WAS USED PRIMARILY TO MAKE SHEETS FOR WRITING, WHICH WERE MADE BY SOAKING THE LEAVES IN WATER AND THEN DRYING THEM IN THE SUN.

I WONDER IF I SHOULD TRY TO GET INSPIRED BY THINKING OF SOMETHING ELSE?

I COULD THINK OF A TART OF SMOKED CHEESE... OR MAYBE OF SOMEONE SPECIAL!

I'VE GOT IT! I'LL PRETEND THE HYMN IS FOR BASTET, BUT IN REALITY I'LL DEDICATE IT TO... *PETUNIA!*

OH, NOBLE FELINE GODDESS, WHEN I LOOK UPON YOU, I THINK, "YOU HAVE EYES THE COLOR OF THE SKY AND A HEART FILLED WITH LOVE..."

MEANWHILE, EVEN TERSILLA HAD HER PAWS IN ACTION...

RAT-KARUE, WE HAVE TO SPEAK! IT'S URGENT!

HORUS' BEAK! I'M RESTING!

80

YOUR REST CAN WAIT! BASTET IS VERY *DISPLEASED* WITH YOU!

-:GULP!:-

THE MONUMENT MUST BE FINISHED WITH THE FACE OF A CAT! OTHERWISE THE GODDESS WILL STOP FAVORING YOU!

BUT, BUT... I CAN'T DO ANYTHING! THE PHARAOH DOESN'T REALLY WANT TO HEAR ANYTHING ABOUT THE FACE OF A CAT!

IF CHEPHREN IS THE OBSTACLE... THE GODDESS ORDERS YOU TO *ELIMINATE* HIM!

WHAAAAAT?

BASTET THINKS YOU'D BE A BETTER PHARAOH THAN HIM!

M-M-ME?

YOU HAVE A DAY TO THINK IT OVER, RAT-KARUE...

WAIT, RAT-SHEPSUT!

REBELLING AGAINST THE PHARAOH IS A RISKY THING TO DO. I COULD LOSE MY FUR!

WHAT ARE YOU WORRYING ABOUT? BASTET IS WITH YOU AND SO YOU'LL WIND UP WITH ALL OF EGYPT!

HMM... FIRST OF ALL, I WILL NEED TO IMPRISON CHEPHREN AND HIS FAMILY!

EASY! THE GODDESS ALREADY KNOWS HOW AND WHERE TO DO IT! LISTEN...

IN THE MEANTIME, WE WENT ON WITH OUR WORK...

➴GRRR➴!

!?

TAKE THIS TASTER AWAY! HE'S DEVOURING ALL OUR SUPPLIES!

➴SLURP!

BAM

HA, HA, HA, HA!

➴OOF➴... HOW LONG DOES IT TAKE?!? WHAT MILK PAP!✽

...

✽HOW BORING!

THE EVENING OF THE GRAND FESTIVAL ARRIVED AND WE FINALLY SAW OUR DEAR FRIEND AGAIN...

RATTY-ATUM!

MY FRIENDS!

THE MOMENT CAME FOR ME TO READ THE HYMN THAT I COMPOSED IN HONOR OF THE GODDESS BASTET.

UMM...

"OH, NOBLE FELINE GODDESS WHEN I LOOK UPON YOU, I THINK: YOU HAVE A FACE OF FONTINA, A NOSE OF SOFT CHEESE..."

~SQUEEAK!~ BUT THIS ISN'T THE TEXT I WROTE!

THIS IS SCANDALOUS!

THE SCRIBE HAS INSULTED THE GODDESS BASTET!

HOW COULD YOU OFFEND BASTET?!

BUT... BUT...

I ASKED YOU TO WRITE A HYMN, NOT INSULTS! YOU SHALL PAY FOR THIS OUTRAGE!

GUARDS, ARREST HIM!

OH, NO! POOR GERON-ANKH-AMON!

THAT HAS YOUR PAW PRINTS ALL OVER IT, HUH? I RECOGNIZE YOUR STYLE...

AT THE START OF THE FESTIVAL, WITHOUT ANYONE NOTICING, WE SUBSTITUTED A PAPYRUS I WROTE IN THE PLACE OF STILTON'S!

HEE, HEE, HEE!

DIVINE PHARAOH, I ASSURE YOU THAT IT WAS AN ERROR!

STOP!

!

IF YOU ARREST HIM, YOU'LL HAVE TO ARREST ME, TOO!

MY VERY DEAR NEPHEW!

AND ME, TOO!

AND ME, TOO!

AND ME, TOO! ONE RAT FOR ALL, ALL RATS FOR ONE!

SO BE IT! THE PRISON AIR WILL TAKE AWAY YOUR DESIRE TO INSULT THE GODS!

THEY DRAGGED US UNDER THE ROYAL PALACE AND LOCKED US UP IN A CELL.

WOULD YOU MIND TELLING ME WHAT YOU HAD IN MIND WHEN YOU WROTE THOSE WORDS?

HOW MANY TIMES DO I HAVE TO KEEP SAYING IT, I DIDN'T WRITE THAT!

THEN WHO COULD IT HAVE BEEN?

~TSK!~

MAYBE YOU WERE THE VICTIM OF THE PIRATE CATS' TRAP!

THAT'S RIGHT!

BUT WE CAN'T PROVE IT! LET'S TRY TO FIND A WAY TO GET OUT OF THIS CELL, INSTEAD!

MAYBE TRAP COULD EAT UP THE PRISON WALLS!

YOU'RE SO FUNNY, COUSIN!

LET'S FEEL THE WALLS! THERE COULD BE A *SECRET PASSAGE!*

KNOCK KNOCK

DON'T DELUDE YOURSELF, *YOU STUPID SQUEAKERS!* YOU'LL NEVER GET OUT OF THIS HOLE!

?!?

THE DANCER? THE PRIESTS?

FINALLY WE MEET! YOU MUST BE...

TERSILLA OF CATATONIA, DAUGHTER OF CATARDONE III!

THE PIRATE CATS... ~*BRRR!*~

I WANT YOU TO KNOW THAT BY TOMORROW, *HISTORY* WILL HAVE CHANGED... IN FAVOR OF CATS, OBVIOUSLY!

DURING HIS ANNUAL JOURNEY DOWN THE NILE, CHEPHREN WILL HAVE AN UNPLEASANT SURPRISE!

WH-WHAT DO YOU MEAN?

THAT THE PHARAOH WILL BE IMPRISONED BY RAT-KARLIE AND FORCED TO SURRENDER HIS REIGN TO THE VIZIER!

THE VIZIER... A TRAITOR?

IMPOSSIBLE!

OH, BUT HE IS! ALL I HAD TO DO TO CONVINCE HIM WAS PROMISE HIM THE TITLE OF PHARAOH!

RIGHT!

YOU'LL NEVER MANAGE TO IMPRISON THE PHARAOH!

IT WAS EASY WITH YOU, MOUSE!

MOLDY MOZZARELLA! WAS IT YOU WHO SUBSTITUTED THE PAPYRUS?!?

NOT TO BOAST...!

NOW I UNDERSTAND! WITH CHEPHREN OUT OF THE WAY, YOU'LL BE ABLE TO GIVE THE SPHINX THE FACE OF A CAT!

YOU GOT IT, **SWEETIE!** THAT WAY WE'LL BECOME POWERFUL AND FAMOUS...

GOODBYE, RATLINGS! I HOPE YOU LIKE YOUR CELL, BECAUSE YOUR ONLY CHANCE OF LEAVING IT...

...WILL BE IF SOME ARCHAEOLOGIST STUMBLES UPON YOU IN A FEW MILLENNIA!

SLAM

WHAT WICKED RATS!

LET'S LOOK FOR A WAY TO GET OUT! WE PROMISED VON VOLT THAT WE'D STOP THE PIRATE CATS AND WE'RE GOING TO SUCCEED!

WE SPENT THE REST OF THE NIGHT LOOKING FOR A WAY TO ESCAPE...

KNOCK KNOCK KNOCK

AND AT THE FIRST LIGHT OF DAWN...

HEY, LISTEN! THIS STONE *ECHOED!*

HEAR THAT?

KNOCK KNOCK

LET ME TRY!

KNOCK KNOCK

WHAM

MAY I COME IN?

RATTY-ATUM?

?!?

WHAT ARE YOU DOING HERE?

I'VE COME TO FREE YOU!

I CAN'T LET MY RESCUERS *ROT* IN PRISON!

YOU'RE A TRUE FRIEND, RATTY-ATUM!

RAT-TASTIC! THERE'S A *SECRET PASSAGE!*

OH, YES, THE PALACE UNDERGROUND IS FULL OF THEM! CHEPHREN'S ANCESTORS HAD THEM BUILT SO THEY COULD ESCAPE AT ANY MOMENT!

THE GODS REALLY WANTED ME TO BE THE ONE IN CHARGE OF LAST YEAR'S RESTORATION WORK!

AND... WHERE DOES THIS PASSAGE GO?

AH, YOU'RE AWAKE NOW, COUSIN!

IT COMES OUT ON THE BANKS OF THE NILE!

THE NILE?

RATTY-ATUM, YOU'VE GOT TO LISTEN TO US... THE PHARAOH IS IN GRAVE DANGER!

~GULP!~

IN SHORT, WE TOLD OUR FRIEND ABOUT THE PIRATE CATS' PLAN...

...LEAVING OUT ONLY THE DETAIL OF TIME TRAVEL.

CATS! I MUST RUN AND SAVE THE PHARAOH!

WE'LL COME, TOO!

MOLDY MOZZARELLA! I'M AFRAID OF TIGHT SPACES!

WATCH YOUR HEADS! THE TUNNEL GETS EVEN NARROWER FARTHER ALONG!

MEANWHILE, CHEPHREN'S SHIP WAS TRAVELING ALONG THE NILE TOWARDS GIZA, THE FIRST STAGE OF A JOURNEY THAT WOULD TAKE THE PHARAOH AND HIS FAMILY TO THE MOUTH OF THE RIVER AT THE MEDITERRANEAN SEA...

THE NILE
IS THE LONGEST RIVER IN THE WORLD: ITS COURSE IS SOME 4,145 MILES LONG (INCLUDING ITS FIRST BRANCH, THE NILE KAGERA), ENDING AT THE MEDITERRANEAN SEA. IN ANTIQUITY, ITS PERIODIC FLOODS MADE THE FIELDS FERTILE SINCE THEY DEPOSITED PRECIOUS MUD SILT ONTO THE GROUND.

WHAT'S GOING ON, MICERINO? YOU'VE BEEN SAD EVER SINCE YESTERDAY EVENING! DO YOU MISS YOUR FRIENDS?

YES, MAMA...

MICERINO, ONE DAY YOU WILL REIGN OVER EVERYTHING IN MY PLACE! YOU MUST LEARN THAT THE PHARAOH CANNOT ALLOW THE GODS TO BE INSULTED!

EXACTLY, CHEPHREN! SO WHY DO YOU CONTINUE TO OPPOSE THE WILL OF BASTET!

RAT-KARUE, HOW DARE YOU ADDRESS ME IN THAT TONE?

I DARE BECAUSE BASTET GAVE ME THE RIGHT TO DO SO!

BASTET? HOLD YOUR TONGUE IF YOU DON'T WANT TO WIND UP LIKE THE SCRIBE AND HIS FRIENDS!

PRIESTS, TELL HIM WHOSE SIDE THE GODDESS IS ON!

ON THAT OF RAT-KARUE... DEAREST EX-PHARAOH!

HEE, HEE, HEE...

WHAT ARE THESE WORDS?

GUARDS, ARREST THE ROYAL FAMILY!

BUT--BUT--

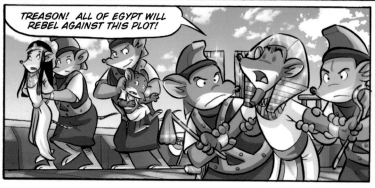

TREASON! ALL OF EGYPT WILL REBEL AGAINST THIS PLOT!

YOU'RE WASTING YOUR BREATH, CHEPHREN... EGYPT WILL ONLY KNOW THAT YOU AND YOUR FAMILY HAD AN ACCIDENT DURING THE TRIP!

EVEN WHEN YOU'RE FAVORED BY THE GODS, IT'S NOT WISE TO SWIM IN A RIVER INFESTED WITH CROCODILES...

-*GRRR*-...
SCOUNDRELS!

NOT FAR AWAY...

WE'VE GOT TO SAIL *FASTER!*

WHAT CAN WE DO?

RIGHT...THIS BOAT IS TOO SLOW!

WE CAN JUMP INTO THE WATER AND PUSH THE BOAT!

WHAT ARE YOU SAYING? THAT'S TOO HARD -- WE CAN'T DO IT!

YOU'RE A REGULAR CHEESE-HEAD! ALL YOU HAVE TO DO IS GRAB THE SHIP AND MOVE YOUR LEGS A BIT!

HMM...

COME ON! IT'S THE ONLY WAY TO GO FASTER!

A LITTLE LATER...

-*PUFF, PANT...*- I CAN'T DO ANYMORE!

BUT I'M DOING IT ALL MYSELF!

COME ON, COUSIN, APPLY SOME GRIT! LEARN FROM THOSE CROCODILES!

HUH?

OWOWOWOW!

IT LOOKS TO ME LIKE STILTON HAS RUINED OUR PLANS ONCE AGAIN!

-HUMPH-... WHICH DO YOU PREFER? PRISON OR WATER?

PRISON!

WATER!

SORRY, DADDY DEAR, BUT THIS TIME BONZO'S RIGHT!

!

THUMP

I HATE WAAAATER!

SPLASH

YOU WON, RATS IN BOOTS! BUT WE'LL SEE EACH OTHER AGAIN SOON -- I SWEAR IT BY THE WORD OF TERSILLA!

THEY ALWAYS MANAGE TO SLIP AWAY!

RIGHT, BUT I'LL BET WE'LL MEET THEM AGAIN!

THANKS, RATTY-ATUM, YOU SAVED ME! HOW DID YOU KNOW THAT--

I'LL EXPLAIN EVERYTHING TO YOU! YOU WON'T BELIEVE YOUR EARS!

WELL, WHERE DID THE TRAITOROUS VIZIER DISAPPEAR?

-SIGH!-

I SPOTTED HIM HIDING AMONG THE EXTRA FRUIT!

95

IN NEW MOUSE CITY, A FRIEND WAS WAITING TO TOAST US WITH CHEESE MOUSSE!

POP

FRIENDS!

PROFESSOR VON VOLT!

COME ON, TELL ME EVERYTHING!

YOUR SUSPICIONS WERE CORRECT: THE CATS' GOAL REALLY WAS THE SPHINX!

THEY WANTED TO GIVE IT THE FACE OF A CAT!

RIGHT, BUT THANKS TO US, IT STILL HAS THE APPEARANCE TODAY THAT WE ALL KNOW!

THE FACE OF THE PHARAOH CHEPHREN!

ALTHOUGH, IF YOU LOOK HARD... YUM, YUM... THE FACE OF THE SPHINX LOOKS A LITTLE FAMILIAR!

FAMILIAR?

YES, IF THE SPHINX HAD A PAIR OF GLASSES, IT WOULD LOOK A LOT LIKE YOU, COUSIN!

?

D-D-DO YOU REALLY THINK SO?

HA, HA, HA!

OF COURSE NOT, I WAS JUST KIDDING!

~SQUEEEEAK!~

SMACK

HA, HA, HA!

MY DEAR RODENT FRIENDS, FAREWELL UNTIL THE NEXT ADVENTURE... ANOTHER WHISKERFUL OF AN ADVENTURE WRITTEN BY STILTON... *Geronimo Stilton!*

IT WAS A BEAUTIFUL MORNING IN NEW MOUSE CITY. A WARM BREEZE WAS BLOWING, GIVING THE CITY A TASTE OF SPRING.

THE COLISEUM CON

BUT THAT VERY MORNING, MY ALARM CLOCK DIDN'T GO OFF AND I WAS *VERY* LATE!

OH, EXCUSE ME, I HAVEN'T INTRODUCED MYSELF YET. MY NAME IS STILTON, GERONIMO STILTON, AND I EDIT THE RODENT'S GAZETTE, THE MOST FAMOUSE PAPER ON MOUSE ISLAND.

SO AS I WAS SAYING, I WAS *RUNNING* WHEN...

-:PUFF! PUFF!:-

SLAM

-:SQUEAK!:-

~SQUEAK!~ MY POOR TAIL!

~SQUEEAK!~ MY POOR PAW!

~SQUEEEAK!~ MY POOR NOSE!

BAM

OOPS!

I FINALLY GOT TO THE OFFICE, BUT MY TROUBLES WEREN'T OVER...

GERONIMO, THERE'S A VERY IMPORTANT VISITOR FOR YOU!

IT WAS THE FAMOUS OPERA SINGER RATIDO DOMINGO!

AH, GOOD MORNING, DR. STILTON!

UM... GOOD MORNING!

I INTEND TO PUBLISH MY BIOGRAPHY AND I WANT YOU TO **write it!**

M-ME?

I GREATLY ADMIRE YOUR BOOKS AND I KNOW YOU'LL BE ABLE TO FIND THE RIGHT WORDS TO DESCRIBE MY ART! LISTEN...

BE GONE, OH RAT! FADE AWAY, MOZZAREL-LA! AT DAWN, I SHALL SQUEAK...!

?!?

IT WAS MY GRANDFATHER, WILLIAM SHORTPAWS, NICKNAMED "TANK"...

UM...HELLO, GRANDPA!

WAKE UP!

HAVE YOU READ THE THE DAILY RAT?

ACTUALLY, THAT'S SALLY RATMOUSEN'S PAPER. MINE'S CALLED...

I KNOW PERFECTLY WELL WHAT THE PAPER I FOUNDED IS CALLED!

THAT RAT'S PAPER HAS AN ARTICLE ON RATIDO DOMINGO'S CONCERT, BUT THERE'S NOTHING ABOUT IT IN THE RODENT GAZETTE!

RATIDO? THAT'S ODD... HE WAS HERE A LITTLE WHILE AGO!

WHAT? AND YOU DIDN'T INTERVIEW HIM?

WHAT DO YOU DO IN YOUR OFFICE, SLEEP? WAKE UUUP!!!

WAKE UP!

WAKE UP!

?!?

?!?

WAKE UUUUP!!!

CRASH

CRASH

CRASH

GRANDSON? ARE YOU STILL THERE? WHAT ARE YOU DOING... ARE YOU REALLY ASLEEP?

AFTER A DAY LIKE THAT, I DIDN'T WANT TO DO ANYTHING BESIDES GO HOME AND NIBBLE ON SOME CRACKERS AND CHEESE...

INSTEAD...

ROTTEN ROQUEFORT! THE REFRIGERATOR'S EMPTY!

~SIGH!~

DEAR COUSIN, I WAS PASSING THROUGH AND GOT HUNGRY! NEXT TIME COULD YOU BUY SOME FRESH MOZZARELLA, TOO? THANKS! TRAP

I WAS ABOUT TO GO LOOK FOR A STORE THAT WAS OPEN, WHEN...

RRINGGRRINGG

MY CELL PHONE?

WHO KNOWS WHO THAT IS? LET'S HOPE IT'S NOT SOMEONE ELSE WHO WANTS TO SCREAM IN MY EAR!

RRINGGRRINGG

H-HELLO?

HELLO, GERONIMO? IT'S AMPY VON VOLT!

AH, GOOD EVENING, PROFESSOR!

SORRY TO DISTURB YOU, BUT YOU MUST COME TO MY LABORATORY RIGHT AWAY!

NOW? TO TELL THE TRUTH, I...

IT'S AN EMERGENCY! THE PIRATE CATS HAVE GONE INTO ACTION!

THE P-P-PIRATE CATS?!?

YES! THE TEMPOGRAPH, THE DEVICE I INVENTED TO MONITOR HISTORY, SHOWS THAT THEY'RE TRAVELING INTO THE PAST!

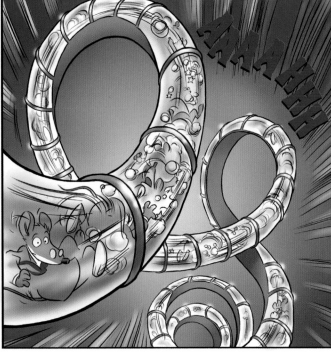

FSSHOOOMM

WUMP!

GERONIMO, ARE YOU OKAY?

~GLUB!~ WHERE AM I?

SORRY ABOUT THE TRIP, BUT CONNECTING YOUR BASEMENT TO MY LABORATORY WAS THE QUICKEST WAY TO GET YOU HERE!

Y-YES, OF COURSE, I UNDERSTAND...

Uncle Geronimo!

BENJAMIN! YOU'RE HERE, TOO?

AND THAT'S ALSO WHY WE'RE HERE!

CIAO, UNCLE G!

THEA! BUGSY WUGSY! THE PROFESSOR CALLED YOU TOO!

I'LL NEED ALL OF YOUR HELP TO FOIL THE PIRATE CATS' PLAN!

DID YOU TAKE A RIDE ON THAT HORRIBLE SLIDE TOO?

NO, YOU'RE THE ONLY LUCKY ONE! THE KIDS AND I WERE "SATISFIED" WITH THE SUBWAY.

AND WHERE'S TRAP?

HE DIDN'T COME. I TRIED TO CALL HIM, BUT I COULDN'T FIND HIM...

MEANWHILE...

OOF... I WAS HOPING GERONIMO'D GONE SHOPPING AGAIN!

TELL US, PROFESSOR, WHAT'S THE PIRATE CATS' DESTINATION THIS TIME AROUND?

THE TEMPOGRAPH SHOWS THAT THEY'RE HEADING TO *ANCIENT ROME*, IN THE YEAR 80 A.D., DURING THE REIGN OF EMPEROR TITUS.

ROME

ACCORDING TO THE LEGEND, THE CITY OF ROME WAS FOUNDED IN AROUND 753 B.C. BY ROMULUS, THE FIRST OF SEVEN KINGS (THE OTHERS WERE, IN ORDER: NUMA POMPILIUS, TULLUS HOSTILLIUS, ANCUS MARCIUS, L. TARQUINIUS PRISCUS, SERVIUS TULLIUS AND TARQUINIUS SUPERBUS). WHEN IT BECAME A REPUBLIC, ROME EXTENDED ITS RULE ACROSS THE ENTIRE BASIN OF THE MEDITERRANEAN SEA AND BECAME THE GREATEST POWER OF THE TIME. AFTER A PERIOD OF CIVIL WAR, GAIUS JULIUS CAESAR OCTAVIUS, CAESAR'S NEPHEW, TOOK POWER, TRANSFORMED THE REPUBLIC INTO AN EMPIRE, AND HAD HIMSELF NAMED AUGUSTUS. THE OFFICIAL LANGUAGE OF ANCIENT ROME WAS LATIN, BUT GREEK WAS ALSO SPOKEN WIDELY.

ROME

FANTASTIC! I'VE ALWAYS DREAMED OF VISITING ANCIENT ROME!

DO YOU HAVE AN IDEA WHY THEY CHOSE THAT YEAR?

WELL, THE ONLY EVENT WORTH MENTIONING...

...IS THE INAUGURATION OF THE FLAVIAN AMPHITHEATER, BETTER KNOWN AS THE COLISEUM!

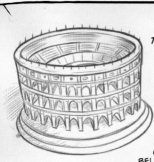

THE FLAVIAN AMPHITHEATER (BETTER KNOWN AS THE COLISEUM)

BEGUN IN AROUND 72 A.D. BY EMPEROR VESPASIAN, THE AMPHITHEATER WAS FINISHED AND INAUGURATED IN AROUND 80 A.D., UNDER EMPEROR TITUS. THE AMPHITHEATER WAS GIVEN THE NAME FLAVIAN IN HONOR OF VESPASIAN AND TITUS, WHO BELONGED TO THE FLAVIAN "GENS" (THAT'S "FAMILY" IN LATIN). THE DERIVATION OF THE NAME "COLISEUM" -- WHICH THE AMPHITHEATER HAS COME TO BE KNOWN BY THROUGHOUT THE WORLD -- IS LESS CERTAIN. ACCORDING TO SOME STORIES, THE NAME COMES FROM THE FACT THAT IN ANCIENT TIMES, A GIGANTIC STATUE OF THE EMPEROR NERO NAMED THE "COLOSSUS NERONIS," -- THAT'S THE "COLOSSUS OF NERO" -- LOOMED NEARBY. MORE THAN 150 FEET TALL AND WITH THREE ROWS OF ARCHES, THE COLISEUM COULD HOLD 50,000 SPECTATORS. INSIDE, THE SO-CALLED "ROMAN CIRCUS" WAS HELD, WHICH HAD GAMES AND ALSO GLADIATORIAL COMBAT -- EVEN SHIP BATTLES (THE AMPHITHEATER WAS FILLED WITH WATER SOMETIMES). IN THE UPPER PART OF THE AMPHITHEATER, THERE WERE WOODEN POLES FOR HOLDING UP CANVAS TENTS, WHICH WERE TO PROTECT SPECTATORS FROM THE SUN. UNDER THE CENTRAL PART OF THE AMPHITHEATER THERE WERE ROOMS AND SUBTERRANEAN CORRIDORS, IN WHICH THE MEN, ANIMALS, AND MACHINERY FOR THE GAMES WERE HIDDEN.

THE COLISEUM? WHAT COULD THE PIRATE CATS DO WITH IT?

MAYBE THEY WANT TO TURN IT INTO A MARBLE URN... HEE HEE HEE!

?!!?

A-A-AM I WRONG OR DID THAT GIFT BOX JUST SP-SP-SPEAK?

SPEAKING OF WHICH... THAT PACKAGE ARRIVED AT THE OFFICE FOR YOU AND I THOUGHT I'D BRING IT HERE.

COULD A SPY FOR THE PIRATE CATS BE HIDING INSIDE IT?

~GULP!~ A SPY...IN MY SECRET LABORATORY!

COME ON, GERONIMO! OPEN IT!

M-ME?

SQUEAK-A-BOO?*

AHHH!

*SURPRISE!

HEY, STILTON-BABY! DID YOU LIKE MY LITTLE JOKE?

HERCULE POIRAT?!?

~MMF! MMF!~

THANK GOODNESS, IT'S YOUR DETECTIVE FRIEND!

HEE, HEE, HEE... HE ADORES PLAYING TRICKS ON PEOPLE!

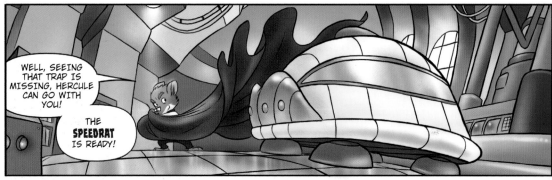

WELL, SEEING THAT TRAP IS MISSING, HERCULE CAN GO WITH YOU!

THE SPEEDRAT IS READY!

BILLIONS OF BUN-CHES OF BANANAS! IS THAT VON VOLT'S TIME MACHINE?

EXACTLY! ARE YOU COMING WITH US?

DO YOU THINK THEA WILL AGREE?

YOU'LL HAVE TO ASK HER...

SO! HAVE YOU TWO DECIDED TO GET ON BOARD?

I'M YOURS TO COMMAND, THEA!

HE'S REALLY IN LOVE!

SO...

I PUT ANCIENT ROMAN *CLOTHING* UNDER THE SEATS...

AND SOME *SESTERCES!*

SESTERCES

IN ANCIENT ROME THERE WERE VARIOUS DIFFERENT COINS: THE AS, SESTERCE (WHICH WAS WORTH ABOUT TWO AND A HALF AS), DENARIUS (WORTH ABOUT FOUR SESTERCES) AND AUREUS (WORTH ABOUT 25 DENARI). EACH EMPEROR HAD HIS OWN IMAGE AND HIS MOST SIGNIFICANT ACCOMPLISHMENTS DEPICTED ON THEM.

MY SPECIAL EARPHONES FOR SPEAKING AND UNDERSTANDING THE LANGUAGE OF THE TIME ARE ON THE DASHBOARD.

THANKS! YOU'LL SEE: WE'LL STOP THE CATS!

YES! WE'LL SAVE HISTORY!

TAKE OFF!

ZZZzKKKRRAAKKK

ZZZZZOOOMM

LET'S HOPE THEY SUCCEED AGAIN THIS TIME...

FSSHOOOMM

WHAT'S GOING ON?

?!?

TRAP? HOW COME YOU'RE HERE?

WHY AM I HERE? I REMEMBER I WAS LOOKING FOR SOME FOOD IN GERONIMO'S BASEMENT AND I CRAWLED INTO A HOLE IN THE WALL...

SPEAKING OF SNACKS... YOU WOULDN'T HAVE SOMETHING TO MUNCH ON, WOULD YOU?

...

IN THE MEANTIME, OTHERS HAVE ALREADY ARRIVED IN ANCIENT ROME...

STEADY AS SHE GOES, BONZO! FOLLOW THE TIBER!

BUT WHERE, TERSILLA? I CAN'T SEE ANYTHING IN THIS MIST!

VRRRRR

THE TIBER

IS A RIVER IN CENTRAL ITALY. IT ORIGINATES ON MT. FUMAIOLO, WHICH IS IN THE APENNINES IN EMILIA-ROMAGNA, AND CROSSES THROUGH THE CITY OF ROME, CONTINUING THEN TO FLOW INTO THE TYRRHENIAN SEA. IT'S ABOUT 400 KILOMETERS LONG. DURING THE TIME OF ANCIENT ROME, THE TIBER WAS A MAJOR ROUTE FOR COMMUNICATION, USED TO TRANSPORT MANY GOODS FROM THE SEA TO ROME, AND CONTINUING INLAND FROM THERE.

SO USE THE RADAR! JUST MAKE SURE YOU DON'T SLAM INTO THE RIVER BANK.

OKAY, OKAY! BUT I DON'T UNDERSTAND WHY IT'S ALWAYS MY TURN TO DRIVE!

BECAUSE I'M CATARDONE, RULER OF THE PIRATE CATS AND SHE'S MY DAUGHTER! DON'T YOU HAVE ANYTHING BETWEEN YOUR EARS?

OW! THAT BLOW'S BETWEEN MY EARS... BUT NOT THE EXPLANATION!

MEOW DOWN*, DADDY DEAR! HERE'S THE CLOACA MAXIMA, ANCIENT ROME'S SEWER SYSTEM! LET'S HIDE THE CATJET HERE!

BLECH, IN THE SEWER? THAT DOESN'T SEEM VERY DIGNIFIED FOR A KING!

QUIET, YOU HAIRBALL

*CALM DOWN

THE CLOACA MAXIMA

ROME IS THE MOST ANCIENT CITY TO HAVE BUILT A NETWORK OF SEWERS FOR DUMPING LIQUID REFUSE. CONSTRUCTED IN THE 6TH CENTURY B.C. BY THE LAST KINGS OF ROME, THE CLOACA MAXIMA WAS DUG OUT BELOW GROUND LEVEL. ORIGINALLY IT WAS AN OPEN-AIR CANAL THAT LIQUID REFUSE WAS THROWN INTO. ONLY LATER WAS IT COVERED OVER.

PULL OVER, BONZO!

TERSILLA, WHY ARE WE IN ANCIENT ROME?

WHAT A STENCH!

SIMPLE, DADDY DEAR...WE'RE GOING TO SEIZE THE COLISEUM!

THE COLISEUM? AND WHAT ARE WE GOING TO DO WITH THE COLISEUM?

MAKE IT INTO A MARBLE RUN!

WOULDN'T YOU LIKE IT IF THEY NAMED THE AMPHITHEATER "CATAR-DONIUS?"

HMM... ACTUALLY, THAT SOUNDS NICE!

YES... FOR A MARBLE RUN!

IF THE COLISEUM HAD YOUR NAME, THE PIRATE CAT LINEAGE WOULD BE FAMOUS THROUGH-OUT THE CENTURIES!

THROUGHOUT THE CENTURIES... AND IN MARBLE MANUALS!

CUT IT OUT WITH THE MARBLE STORY!

-GULP!-

GO ON! I IMAGINE YOU'VE ALREADY THOUGHT OF A PLAN...

YES, DADDY, I'VE THOUGHT OF EVERYTHING! I'LL TELL YOU THE DETAILS ON THE WAY!

AH, IF IT WEREN'T FOR ME!

COME ON, LET'S PUT ON OUR MOUSE MASKS AND DISGUISE OUR-SELVES AS ANCIENT ROMANS!

A FEW MINUTES LATER...

PERFECT! DRESSED LIKE THIS, WE CAN MOVE AROUND UNDIS-TURBED!

WAIT A MINUTE.... WHY ARE YOUR TUNICS ELEGANT AND MINE ALL RATTY?

BECAUSE CATARDONE AND I ARE GOING TO PRETEND TO BE TWO RICH ROMANS FROM THE PROVINCES AND YOU'RE GOING TO GET HIRED AS A WORKER AT THE COLISEUM!

A WORKER? BUT I DON'T WANT TO WORK!

YOU ARE SUCH A TAIL SMASHER!* STOP IT AND LET'S GET MOVING!

-SIGH!-

*A PAIN

110

SUCH TRAFFIC! I DIDN'T THINK ROME WOULD BE SO CROWDED!

STOP YOUR BELLYACHING, BONZO, WE'RE THERE!

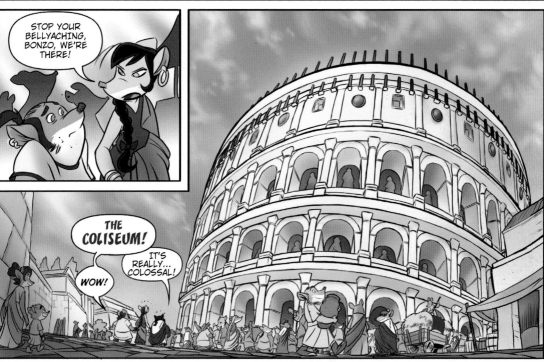

THE COLISEUM!

WOW!

IT'S REALLY... COLOSSAL!

NOW THAT WE'RE HERE, WHAT ARE WE GOING TO DO?

BONZO WILL GET HIRED AS A WORKER WHILE YOU AND I WILL GO FIND EMPEROR TITUS!

WE'LL SEE THAT WE BECOME HIS FRIENDS AND ATTEND THE INAUGURATION OF THE COLISEUM...

HEE, HEE, HEE... AND THEN WHAT DO YOU HAVE IN MIND, TERSILLA?

I REALLY HAVE TO EXPLAIN EVERYTHING TO YOU, HUH?

UM... NO, I GET WHAT YOUR PLAN IS... BONZO, LET'S SEE IF YOU KNOW IT, TOO!

?

UM, LET'S SEE...DURING THE INAUGURATION, I WILL PRETEND TO ATTACK THE EMPEROR...

...SO CATARDONE WILL BE ABLE TO PRETEND TO SAVE HIM AND THEN, IN REWARD, ASK TITUS TO NAME THE COLISEUM AFTER HIM!

WHAT ARE YOU LOOKING AT ME LIKE THAT FOR, TERSILLA? DID I SAY SOMETHING RATICULOUS*?

*RIDICULOUS

NO, NO, THAT'S REALLY THE PLAN! I'M SURPRISED THAT YOU FIGURED IT OUT YOURSELF!

SO, CAN I BE A RICH ROMAN, TOO?

TRIM YOUR SAILS*, BONZO, YOU HAVE TO BE AT THE COLISEUM AND FIND A JOB WHERE YOU CAN ATTACK TITUS!

*DON'T GET FULL OF YOURSELF

A LITTLE LATER...

NAME AND **ADDRESS.**

CAIUS BONZUS. ADDRESS... CLOACA MAXIMA!

GOOD, BONZO'S BEEN HIRED! WE CAN GO TO THE IMPERIAL PALACE!

MAKE WAY, MAKE WAY! LET THE GREAT TITUS PASS THROUGH!

?!?

THE EMPEROR?

WHAT'S HE DOING HERE?

I DON'T KNOW, DADDY DEAR, BUT GET READY...

READY FOR WHAT?

TO MEET THE EMPEROR!

WOMP

~GULP!~

CRASH

DIVINE EMPEROR!

BY JUPITER'S BEARD!

EMPEROR TITUS

THE EMPEROR'S FULL NAME WAS TITUS FLAVIUS VESPASIANUS BUT HE CAME TO BE CALLED JUST TITUS IN ORDER TO DISTINGUISH HIM FROM HIS FATHER, WHO HAD THE SAME NAME AND WENT DOWN IN HISTORY AS VESPASIAN. TITUS WAS AN EMPEROR GREATLY LOVED BY HIS PEOPLE. HIS POLICIES WERE INSPIRED BY THE PRINCIPLES OF LEGALITY, GENEROSITY, AND MERCY: DURING HIS ENTIRE REIGN (79 A.D.–81 A.D.) TITUS AVOIDED WIELDING THE DEATH PENALTY, WHICH WAS IN FORCE AT THAT TIME.

HOW DARE YOU THREATEN THE EMPEROR, YOU MOUSE MONGREL!

~GULP!~

STOP! STOP! THERE'S BEEN A MISTAKE!

FORGIVE MY FATHER'S CLUMSINESS! HE DIDN'T MEAN TO DO YOU ANY HARM!

WHO ARE YOU?

MY NAME IS LICINIA MOUSILLA AND HE IS CATARDONIUS CATARDICUS. WE BELONG TO A NOBLE FAMILY THAT LIVES IN ALEXANDRIA IN EGYPT!

IN ALEXANDRIA? THAT CITY IS VERY DEAR TO MY FAMILY... MY FATHER WAS THERE WHEN HE WAS CHOSEN EMPEROR!

OH, I KNOW IT! I KNOW IT VERY WELL!

PRAETORIANS! LET THAT RODENT GO!

AS YOU WISH, EMPEROR!

-PHEW!-

THE PRAETORIANS

THE PRAETORIAN GUARD WAS ORGANIZED BY EMPEROR AUGUSTUS (WHO RULED FROM 27 B.C.-14 A.D.) AND PERMANENTLY FOUNDED BY HIS SUCCESSOR, TIBERIUS (WHO RULED FROM 14 A.D.-37 A.D.). THE PRAETORIANS' PRIMARY TASK WAS TO PROTECT THE EMPEROR, BUT THEY ALSO PERFORMED ADMINISTRATIVE TASKS AND SECRET MISSIONS.

TELL ME, WHAT BRINGS YOU TO ROME?

WE'RE HERE TO SEE THE INAUGURATION OF THE AMPHITHEATER!

YOU UNDERTOOK A VERY LONG AND TIRING JOURNEY. YOUR CURIOSITY DESERVES TO BE REWARDED!

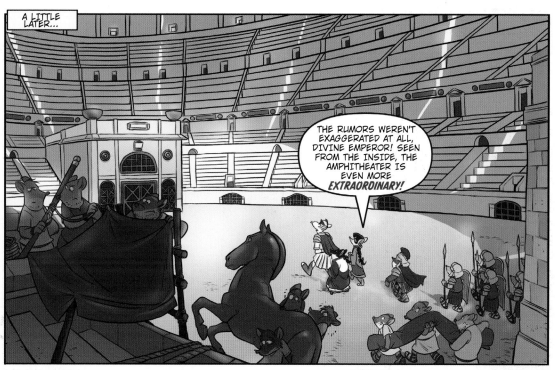

A LITTLE LATER...

THE RUMORS WEREN'T EXAGGERATED AT ALL, DIVINE EMPEROR! SEEN FROM THE INSIDE, THE AMPHITHEATER IS EVEN MORE *EXTRAORDINARY!*

THE CREDIT BELONGS TO HIM: THE ARCHITECT, FLAVIANUS RATICUM!

AVE, TITUS!*

*HAIL

YOU ARE VERY GENEROUS! BUT THE PRAISE SHOULD GO TO THE WORKERS!

WITHOUT THEIR SKILL, NOTHING WOULD'VE BEEN POSSIBLE!

EVEN THE NEW WORKERS ARE BEHAVING WELL?

YES! ALL OF THEM, EXCEPT FOR A STRANGE RODENT WHO JUST GOT HERE TODAY!

?!?

DURING THE WORK BREAK, HE CARVED LITTLE SPHERES OUT OF STONE AND STARTED TO PLAY WITH THEM!

THERE HE IS! THERE'S NO WAY TO GET HIM TO STOP!

ANYHOW, YOU'LL BE ABLE TO INAUGURATE THE AMPHITHEATER WITHIN A WEEK, AS PLANNED!

EXCELLENT! ROME AWAITS THE INAUGURATION WITH IMPATIENCE!

CATARDONIUS, LICINIA, COME... WHILE WE'RE WAITING FOR THE BIG DAY, I WOULD BE HAPPY TO WELCOME YOU AT THE PALACE!

THANK YOU, EMPEROR!

IF YOU DON'T STOP PLAYING WITH MARBLES, I'LL SOAK YOU, YOU FURBALL! *

OW!

BONK

*TEACH YOU A LESSON

116

FINALLY, WE ALSO ARRIVED IN ANCIENT ROME...

A FEW MORE DRY BRANCHES AND THE SPEEDRAT WILL BE COMPLETELY CAMOUFLAGED!

IS THIS BUSH OKAY, THEA?

LOOK OUT: THAT'S A NETTLE! AND TAKE THAT THING OFF YOUR HEAD. IN THIS PERIOD, THOSE HATS DIDN'T EVEN EXIST YET!

I'M KEEPING MY HAT: IT'S A PRESENT FROM MY GRANDMA. BUT IF YOU ASK ME TO DO IT...

HEE, HEE!

WELL DONE! AND NOW LET'S GET GOING! THE PIRATE CATS ALREADY HAVE ENOUGH OF A LEAD ON US!

TRACKING THEM DOWN IN A CITY AS BIG AS ROME ISN'T GOING TO BE EASY!

MAYBE IT WOULD BE BETTER TO SPLIT UP INTO TWO LITTLE GROUPS TO SEARCH!

RIGHT! YOU AND GERONIMO WILL GO TO THE COLISEUM: ITS INAUGURATION IS OUR ONLY TRAIL.

MEANWHILE THE KIDS AND I WILL SEARCH THE CITY!

A LITTLE LATER...

SEE YOU THIS EVENING AT THE COLISEUM!

OKAY! CIAO!

SHE'S REALLY *pretty*, EH?

INDEED! SHE'S A FASCINATING CITY!

TEE, HEE, HEE...WHAT WERE YOU THINKING OF, STILTON-BABY? I WAS REFERRING TO THEA!

AH... CERTAINLY. MY SISTER IS REALLY A FASCINATING RODENT!

A HALF HOUR LATER, IN FRONT OF THE COLISEUM...

HOW CAN WE SEARCH WITHOUT BEING NOTICED?

WE CAN GET HIRED AS WORKERS AT THE AMPHITHEATER! IT'LL BE EASIER TO KEEP AN EYE ON THE SITUATION FROM THE INSIDE!

YOU'RE RIGHT! LET'S ASK THAT RODENT IF THERE ARE ANY JOBS!

HELLO, MY NAME IS STILTONIUS, GERONIMUS STILTONIUS, AND HE IS MY FRIEND HERCULIUS POIRATUS. WE'D LIKE...

IF YOU'RE LOOKING FOR WORK, I'M SORRY: WE'RE ALL FULL!

OH, NO! NOW WHAT?

LUCIUS, DID I HEAR RIGHT? THESE TWO ARE LOOKING FOR **WORK**?

YES, RATICUM!

YOU SEEM LIKE STRONG RODENTS! YOU'LL DO FINE!

COME WITH ME!

THANKS!

I'D LIKE YOU TO SUBSTITUTE FOR CAIUS BONZUS! INSTEAD OF WORKING, HE SPENDS THE DAY PLAYING WITH MARBLES!

?!?

I KNEW I'D PLAY WITH MARBLES!

JUST HAVE HIM TELL YOU WHAT HIS JOB WAS!

I DIDN'T KNOW THAT THE ANCIENT ROMANS USED TO PLAY WITH marbles!

WHO KNOWS?

UMM...AVE!

AVE!

!!!

AAAHHHHHHH

WHAT GOT INTO HIM?

I DON'T KNOW. THAT RODENT IS VERY STRANGE!

STRANGE! IT'S AS IF...

HERCULE?

WHERE ARE YOU, HERCULE?

HEE, HEE, HEE!

!!!

MMF, MMF...G-G-GERONIMO STILTON! I HAVE TO WARN TERSILLA AND CATARDONE IMMEDIATELY!

MEANWHILE, THEA, BENJAMIN, AND PANDORA...

WHAT A LOT OF PEOPLE ARE HERE AT THE market!

ALL THIS WALKING AROUND HAS MADE ME AS HUNGRY AS A HOUSECAT!

ME, TOO!

WHAT DO YOU THINK ABOUT LUNCH IN A TAVERNA...HUH?

DO YOU SMELL THAT AROMA?

BLECH! IT SEEMS LIKE THE SMELL OF HERRINGS!

HERRINGS FROM THE GATTICO SEA, TO BE PRECISE! AND WHERE THERE'S THAT SMELL, THERE'S USUALLY A CAT!

STRANGE, I STARTED TO SMELL IT WHEN THAT MATRON PASSED NEAR ME!

I SUSPECT THAT...

MATRONS

IN ANCIENT ROME, LADIES WERE CALLED MATRONS. BY LAW, WOMEN WERE ECONOMICALLY DEPENDENT ON THEIR FATHERS, HUSBANDS, OR CLOSEST MALE RELATIVES. THEY HAD NO RIGHTS BUT WERE VERY WELL RESPECTED AND LISTENED TO WITHIN THE FAMILY.

MAYBE, ROME ISN'T AS BIG AS WE THOUGHT AFTER ALL. LET'S FOLLOW HER!

WE HAVE TO BE CAREFUL NOT TO BE NOTICED!

HEY, WHERE'D SHE DISAPPEAR TO?

?!?

HERE I AM!

SPRIZZ

WHAT A STINK! BUT...THAT'S NO LONGER THE SMELL FROM BEFORE...I FEEL LIKE I'M PASSING OUT...

KOFF KOFF KOFF

HEE, HEE, HEE...

IT WAS A GOOD IDEA TO BRING THIS POLECAT ESSENCE TO STUN THOSE SNOOPS WITH! I'M REALLY CURIOUS TO SEE WHO THEY ARE!

→GASP!← THAT'S IMPOSSIBLE: GERONIMO STILTON'S RELATIVES!

I WONDER HOW THEY ALWAYS KNOW WHERE WE ARE!

HUH? FOOTSTEPS!

→PUFF... PANT...←

BONK

BONZO?!

T-TERSILLA?

WHAT'RE YOU DOING HERE? WHY AREN'T YOU AT THE COLISEUM?

TO WARN YOU OF A GREAT DANGER! STILTON...

YES, I KNOW! THE STILTON FAMILY IS IN ROME!

→GULP!← YOU DIDN'T DO TOO BADLY WITH THOSE THREE!

DID YOU FIND A PLACE WHERE YOU CAN TRY TO AMBUSH TITUS?

YES, YES... I'LL HIDE MYSELF UNDER HIS BOX!

PERFECT!

HOW COME YOU'RE NOT WITH CATARDONE?

THEY WERE FILLING MY EARS* AT THE PALACE! CATARDONE AND TITUS WERE DOING NOTHING BUT REMINISCING...

*I WAS BORED

"...ABOUT THEIR YOUTHFUL HEROIC EXPLOITS!"

ONCE I ATTACKED A SHIP WITH A SUBMARINE!

A SUBMARINE? WHAT'S THAT?

WHAT SHOULD WE DO WITH THESE THREE RODENTS?

LOOK FOR SOME ROPE AND A BIGA. WE'LL TAKE THEM TO THE CATJET!

A BIGA

WAS A SMALL TWO-WHEELED CHARIOT THAT WAS USUALLY PULLED BY TWO HORSES. WHEN FOUR HORSES PULLED THE SAME CART INSTEAD, IT WAS CALLED A QUADRIGA. IN ADDITION TO BEING USED FOR REGULAR TRANSPORTATION, BIGAS WERE USED FOR RACES IN THE AMPHITHEATER.

HEE, HEE, HEE... THIS TIME I'VE GOT YOU IN THE PADS OF MY PAWS, GERONIMO STILTON!

THAT EVENING...

YOU'RE REALLY HOPELESS AT MARBLES! I WON EVERY TIME!

IT'S NOT MY FAULT THAT THE MARBLES WERE MADE OF STONE AND HURT MY FINGERS WHEN THEY HIT!

ACTUALLY, DIDN'T THAT CAIUS BONZUS' BEHAVIOR SEEM SUSPICIOUS TO YOU?

RIGHTRIGHTRIGHT...AS SOON AS HE SAW US, HE DASHED AWAY!

PERHAPS HE WAS ONE OF THE PIRATE CATS DRESSED AS A RODENT!

WHAT?!?

BUT...THEN, WE HAVE TO CHASE AFTER HIM!

WHY?

THE FACT THAT HE WAS HERE MEANS THE PIRATE CATS REALLY ARE AIMING FOR THE COLISEUM, SO THEY'LL BE BACK!

THINK SO?

YES, IF WE PRETEND WE DIDN'T RECOGNIZE HIM, HE'LL LEAD US TO HIS PALS IN DUE TIME!

THEA AND THE KIDS ARE LATE! I HOPE NOTHING'S HAPPENED TO THEM!

WHAT ARE YOU WORRIED ABOUT? YOUR SISTER HAS A BLACK BELT IN KARATE

I KNOW, BUT...

CLOMP CLOMP CLOMP

!?

SQUEAK!

SWISH

!?

WAK

OUCH!

AND WHAT'S THIS?

BY THE FLEA-RIDDEN FUR OF A WERECAT!

125

HERCULE, LISTEN: "STILTON, YOUR SISTER AND THE KIDS ARE OUR PRISONERS! IF YOU WANT TO SEE THEM AGAIN SAFE AND SOUND, DON'T POKE YOUR NOSE INTO THE INAUGURATION OF THE COLISEUM! SIGNED: THE PIRATE CATS!"

BILLIONS OF BUNCHES OF BANANAS!

HURRY, STILTON-BABY, WE HAVE TO STOP THAT BIGA!

≂PUFF≂... IT'S GOING TOO FAST. WE'LL NEVER CATCH UP ON FOOT!

!

HOP ON BOARD, STILTON-BABY!

BUT...BUT... WE CAN'T STEAL IT!

WE'RE NOT STEALING IT; WE'RE JUST BORROWING IT... Y-YAAAHH!

MY BIGA! STOP, THIEF! STOP, THIEF!

HURRY, HERCULE!

126

THOSE RODENTS WON'T BE A PROBLEM ANY MORE!

EVERYTHING WHERE IT BELONGS, STILTON-BABY?

MOSTLY...

MY BIGA! MY BIGA!

UH-OH!

WE HAVE TO REPAY THAT RODENT FOR HIS BIGA!

LEAVE HIM A FEW SESTERCES, AND NOW... LET'S *SCRAM*

A LITTLE LATER, IN A TAVERNA...

→SOB!← HOW WILL WE GET BACK THEA, BENJAMIN, AND BUGSY?

TAVERNAS

IN ANCIENT ROME, THERE WERE MANY TAVERNAS, OFTEN LOCATED IN THE WORST AREAS OF THE CITY -- WHERE YOU COULD EAT DISHES WITH POLENTA, SPELT, BARLEY, AND VEGETABLES IN THEM. BESIDES THESE TAVERNS, THERE WERE ALSO THERMOPOLIAS, PLACES WHERE YOU COULD BUY HOT FOOD TO TAKE AWAY, LIKE MODERN TAKE-OUT FOOD.

DON'T CRY, STILTON-BABY!

EAT YOUR CABBAGE SOUP...

I'M NOT HUNGRY!

THIS SOUP MAY NOT BE VERY GOOD, BUT IF YOU WANT TO RESCUE THEA AND THE KIDS, YOU HAVE TO BE IN GOOD SHAPE!

RESCUE THEM? HOW? WE DON'T EVEN KNOW WHERE THE PIRATE CATS ARE HOLDING THEM PRISONER!

THAT'S TRUE, BUT IT'S CLEAR FROM THEIR LETTER THAT THOSE SCOUNDRELS INTEND TO MAKE THEIR MOVE ON THE DAY OF THE INAUGURATION!

IF WE'D ONLY MANAGED TO SEE THE FACES OF THOSE TWO IN THE BIGA, WE'D BE ABLE TO REC-OGNIZE THEM!

WE'VE STILL GOT CAIUS BONZUS!

GIVEN THAT HE'S REALLY A CAT, DO YOU THINK WE'LL SEE HIM AGAIN AT THE COLISEUM AFTER TONIGHT?

UMM... NO!

WE'RE UP A CREEK, HUH?

I'M AFRAID SO!

MEANWHILE, AT THE IMPERIAL PALACE...

TERSILLA, WHERE DID YOU END UP? THE EMPEROR WAS WAITING FOR THE BANQUET!

CALL ME MOUSILLA, DADDY DEAR. SOMEONE MIGHT HEAR YOU!

IS EVERYTHING GOING WELL WITH TITUS?

OH, YES, WE'RE INSEPARABLE NOW!

THIS MORNING I EVEN GOT TO GO TO THE THERMAL BATHS WITH HIM... A TERRIBLE PLACE FOR A CAT!

THERMAL BATHS

IN ANCIENT ROME, THE THERMAL BATHS WERE PUBLIC BUILDINGS EQUIPPED WITH WASHROOMS, AND WERE ONE OF THE MAIN PLACES WHERE ALL CITIZENS COULD BE FOUND. BESIDES NUMEROUS POOLS FOR TAKING BATHS --WITH HOT, WARM, AND COLD WATER-- CHANGING ROOMS, SAUNAS, GYMS, AND, IN THE RICHER BATHS, EVEN THEATERS AND LIBRARIES.

"FIRST THEY TRIED TO BOIL ME IN A TYPE OF SAUNA...

...THEN I ALMOST *DROWNED* IN A POOL FULL OF WATER..."

...AND FINALLY A MASSEUR TRIED TO **DESTROY** MY BACK!"

I WAS SUCH A DEAD WEIGHT THEY HAD TO LOAD ME ONTO A SEDAN-CHAIR TO GO BACK TO THE PALACE!

TSK...DID ANYTHING ELSE HAPPEN?

AH, YES, I ALMOST FORGOT ABOUT THIS. TITUS PROPOSED THAT I BECOME A SENATOR!

SENATOR? BUT THAT'S A VERY IMPORTANT OFFICE!!!

THE SENATE
WAS THE MOST IMPORTANT ASSEMBLY IN ANCIENT ROME. THE TERM, SENATE, COMES FROM THE LATIN WORD, "SENEX," WHICH MEANS "OLD." AS A MATTER OF FACT, IT WAS RECOGNIZED THAT OLD PEOPLE HAD THE EXPERIENCE NEEDED TO MAKE IMPORTANT DECISIONS. FOR THIS REASON, THEREFORE, TO BECOME A SENATOR, BESIDES BEING OF NOBLE ORIGINS, A PERSON HAD TO BE OVER 43.

YOU DID A GOOD JOB, DADDY DEAR! LISTEN, I ALSO HAVE SOME NEWS...

BRIEFLY...

AREN'T YOU AFRAID THAT STILTON WILL BE ABLE TO HINDER MY...UM, OUR... PLAN?

NO, HE WON'T DARE COME NEAR THE COLISEUM AS LONG AS WE HAVE HIS FRIENDS AS HOSTAGES!

FOR SECURITY, I'VE ORDERED BONZO TO STAND GUARD ON THE CATJET!

BUT...I THOUGHT HE WAS GOING TO BE WORKING INSIDE THE AMPHITHE-ATER.

IT'S BETTER IF HE STAYS HIDDEN FOR NOW: STILTON WOULD BE ABLE TO RECOGNIZE HIM! HE'LL COME FOR THE INAUGURATION OF THE COLISEUM!

I HOPE HE DOESN'T MESS UP AT THE CATJET!

COME ON, DADDY DEAR! HE WON'T BE ABLE TO DO THAT...

"...HE JUST HAS TO KEEP HIS EYES OPEN!"

ZZZZZ

ZZZZZ

THE FOLLOWING DAY, HERCULE AND I MOVED AROUND IN ROME, UNDECIDED ABOUT WHAT TO DO...

WE ABSOLUTELY HAVE TO FIND A WAY TO RESCUE THEA AND THE KIDS...

AND FOIL THE PIRATE CATS' PLAN.

RIGHT!

BILLIONS OF BUNCHES OF BANANAS! DID YOU SEE HOW MANY RODENTS ARE IN FRONT OF THE COLISEUM?

THEY'RE ALL HERE FOR THE INAUGURATION! WHAT A MESS!

WE HAVE TO COME UP WITH AN IDEA!

MAYBE WE CAN TRY TO TRAP THE PIRATE CATS IN FRONT OF THE AMPHITHEATER...

AND FORCE THEM TO SHOW US WHERE OUR FRIENDS ARE!

HMM...

REMEMBER THEY'RE WEARING MOUSE MASKS! IT'LL BE HARD TO RECOGNIZE THEM!

STILTONIUS SQUEAKIUS, WHAT A PLEASURE TO SEE YOU!

UMMM... AVE, ARCHITECT RATICUM!

AVE!

DID YOU COME FOR THE INAUGURATION, TOO?

WELL, HERE'S...

AND CAIUS BONZUS? HAVE YOU NEWS OF HIM, BY CHANCE? I HAVEN'T SEEN HIM SINCE YESTERDAY!

TO TELL THE TRUTH...

POOR GUY, I HOPE HE DIDN'T GET SICK...HE SAID HE LIVED AT THE CLOACA MAXIMA...AND IT'S CERTAINLY NOT A VERY HEALTHY PLACE TO LIVE...

!?

!?

BONZUS LIVES IN THE CLOACA **MAXIMA?!?**

YES, THAT'S THE ADDRESS HE GAVE WHEN HE WAS HIRED!

HE'S REALLY A BIZARRE GUY, ACTUALLY MOUSE! OUT OF MANY PLACES, HE PICKED THE MOST...

BUT... WHERE DID THEY GO?

RUN, STILTON-BABY! RUN!

IN THE MEANTIME, AT THE PALACE...

ONLY A FEW MORE HOURS UNTIL THE COLISEUM WILL BE MINE!

OURS, DADDY DEAR, OURS!

WHEN BONZO PRETENDS TO ATTACK THE EMPEROR, I SUGGEST YOU BE THE FIRST TO SPRING TO HIS DEFENSE!

I'LL BE THE SPRINGIEST! BONZO WON'T GET AWAY!

DON'T HURT HIM; JUST MAKE HIM RUN AWAY!

OOF! NOT EVEN A KICK TO THE END OF HIS TAIL!

NOT EVEN THAT!

FINALLY WE ARRIVED AT THE CLOACA MAXIMA.

THIS WAY!

BRRR...THIS DARK *SEWER* GIVES ME THE JITTERS...

TO SAY NOTHING OF THE *STINK* HERE!

LOOK OVER THERE, STILTON-BABY!

THAT MUST BE THE PIRATE CATS' TIME MACHINE! YOU WERE RIGHT TO SUSPECT CAIUS BONZUS!

WE HAVE TO BE QUIET!

I'LL BE AS QUIET AS A MOUSE!

LUCKILY THERE DOESN'T SEEM TO BE ANYONE IN THE NEIGHBORHOOD!

BONK

!

THEA?!?

HERCULE?!?

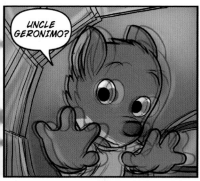

UNCLE GERONIMO?

UH?

BENJAMIN, I'M SO HAPPY TO SEE YOU AGAIN!

ME, TOO, UNCLE GERONIMO!

SORRY ABOUT HITTING YOU, LITTLE BROTHER. I WAS AFRAID YOU WERE THE PIRATE CATS!

IT DOESN'T MATTER! THE IMPORTANT THING IS THAT YOU'RE SAFE AND SOUND!

TELL ME, BUGSY-BABY, HOW DID YOU GET YOURSELVES FREE?

THEA DESERVES THE CREDIT! SHE UNTIED OUR ROPES AND PUT THAT CHEESEHEAD WATCHING US OUT OF ACTION.

IT WASN'T HARD: HE WAS *ASLEEP!*

AND WHERE'S HE NOW?

HERE!

MMMM!

THERE'S NOT A MINUTE TO LOSE! WE'VE GOT TO GO TO THE COLISEUM! THE OTHER PIRATE CATS WILL BE READY TO STRIKE!

FIRST, LET'S QUESTION THIS SCOUNDREL TO FIND OUT THEIR PLAN!

I ALREADY DID THAT! I QUESTIONED HIM WHEN I WAS TYING HIM UP!

THEA QUICKLY BROUGHT US UP TO SPEED ABOUT EVERYTHING...

WITHOUT THEIR ACCOMPLICE, TERSILLA AND CATARDONE CAN'T PUT THEIR PLAN INTO ACTION...

RIGHT, BUT WE'D BETTER NOT RELY ON THAT: TERSILLA COULD MAKE UP ANOTHER PLAN ON THE SPOT! WE'D BETTER GO TO THE COLISEUM, ANYHOW, AND UNMASK THEM!

AND WHAT SHOULD WE DO WITH BONZO?

I'D SAY WE SHOULD LEAVE HIM HERE!

YES, BUT FIRST I WANT TO CHECK HOW...

~SQUEAK!~

SGNACT

HURRY UP! WE HAVE TO STOP HIM BEFORE HE MANAGES TO GET FREE!

GET GOING, STILTON-BABY!

NNNGG!

MEANWHILE, AT THE COLISEUM, EVERYONE WAS WAITING FOR THE ENTRANCE OF THE EMPEROR, SO THAT THE HUNDRED DAYS OF SPECTACLES THAT HAD BEEN ANNOUNCED TO CELEBRATE ITS CONSTRUCTION COULD GET UNDERWAY...

TITUS!

TITUS!

TITUS!

TITUS!

TITUS!

TITUS!

TITUS!

TITUS!

TITUS!

136

THE INAUGURATION OF THE COLISEUM

WAS A MEMORABLE EVENT IN ROMAN HISTORY. IN FACT, TITUS ORDERED IT TO BE CELEBRATED BY A HUNDRED DAYS OF SPECTACLES, WHICH ENTERTAINED THE PUBLIC FROM MORNING UNTIL EVENING. THE EMPEROR NOT ONLY WANTED TO GIVE HIS FAMILY'S NAME PRESTIGE, BUT ALSO TO WIN THE PEOPLE'S AFFECTION.

THIS DAY WILL GO DOWN IN HISTORY!

YOU'RE RIGHT, DEAR TITUS, BUT NOT IN THE WAY YOU THINK!

GET READY TO SPRING TO THE EMPEROR'S DEFENSE!

I'LL BE THE SPRINGIEST!

LET'S HOPE THAT BONZO GETS HERE IN TIME AND THAT THERE'S NO MORE NEWS SINCE YESTER-DAY...

SPRINGIEST! SPRINGIEST!

MEANWHILE, BONZO...

—:PUFF, PANT!:—

—:PUFF!:—

LOOK! BONZO'S CLIMBING ON THE PLATFORMS!

WELL, RATICUM! COULD YOU TELL ME WHAT ALL THESE RODENTS ARE DOING HERE?

TRULY, I...

-GULP!- GERONIMO STILTON?!?

UH-OH!

FORGIVE THE INTRUSION, EMPEROR... BUT I MUST UNMASK THESE SCOUNDRELS!

MEOW!

BY JUPITER'S BEARD! CATARDONIUS IS..IS...A CAT?!

HOW IS THAT POSSIBLE?!?

HIS DAUGHTER MOUSILLA AND CAIUS BONZUS ARE TOO!

GRRR... YOU'RE NOT GOING TO GET US SO EASILY!

THEY'RE ESCAPING!

THUD!

MIAOOWWW!

SBAM

INCREDIBLE! THEY MANAGED TO GET AWAY AGAIN!

THEY ESCAPED RIGHT OUT FROM UNDER OUR NOSES!

VICTORY IS YOURS, STILTON! BUT SOONER OR LATER WE'LL MEET AGAIN!

SO HERE WE ARE AT THE END OF OUR ADVENTURE. ONCE AGAIN, WE'D PREVENTED THE PIRATE CATS FROM CHANGING HISTORY!

IT'S ALL YOUR FAULT, BONZO! IF I CATCH YOU, I'M GOING TO REDRAW THE SPOTS ON YOUR FUR!*

BUT, TERSILLA... I...

*TEACH YOU A LESSON!

LEAVING OUT THE DETAILS OF OUR TRIP THROUGH TIME, I TOLD THE EMPEROR THE WHOLE TRUTH ABOUT THE NEFARIOUS INTENTIONS OF CATARDONIUS, MOUSILLA, AND CAIUS BONZUS!

AND THAT'S THE STORY!

WHAT SCOUNDRELS!

THE EMPEROR WAS SO TAKEN BY OUR COURAGE THAT HE INVITED US TO WATCH THE INAUGURATION OF THE COLISEUM FROM HIS BOX...

..AND THAT EVENING HE WANTED US TO BE THE GUESTS OF HONOR AT A GRAND BANQUET!

THE NEXT DAY, WE SAID GOODBYE TO OUR NEW FRIEND. AFTER SO MUCH DANGER...

FAREWELL, FRIENDS!

...WE COULDN'T WAIT TO GET BACK HOME!

THERE YOU ARE!

Geronimo!

PROFESSOR VOLT!

COME ON, TELL ME EVERYTHING!

YOU'RE NOT GOING TO BELIEVE YOUR EARS!

A LITTLE LATER...

HMMM... WHO KNOWS IF TITUS WOULD HAVE GRANTED THE PIRATE CATS' WISH TO NAME THE AMPHITHEATER AFTER CATARDONIUS...

LUCKILY, WE'LL NEVER KNOW!

ANYWAY, I'M SURE THOSE CHEESEHEADS WILL BE AT IT AGAIN VERY SOON!

RIGHT!

BY THE WAY, THERE COULD BE ANOTHER MISSION I WANT TO ENTRUST YOU WITH!

ANOTHER?

BUT WE JUST GOT BACK!

OH, NO, SORRY, YOU MISUNDER-STOOD ME. IT'S NOT ABOUT THE PIRATE CATS...EVEN THOUGH I MUST ADMIT IT'S A RATHER DELICATE TASK!

COME ON, PROFESSOR! DON'T KEEP US ON TENTERHOOKS!

I IMPLORE YOU: YOU ABSOLUTELY HAVE TO SAVE MY REFRIGERATOR FROM YOUR COUSIN! HE ARRIVED HERE AS SOON AS YOU LEFT... AND HE'S DONE NOTHING BUT EAT!

TRAP?

~BURP!~ WELCOME BACK, COUSINS! DOES ANYONE HAPPEN TO HAVE AN AFTER-DINNER MINT?

MY DEAR RODENT FRIENDS, FAREWELL UNTIL THE NEXT ADVENTURE...ANOTHER WHISKERFUL OF AN ADVENTURE, WRITTEN BY STILTON...
Geronimo Stilton!

Welcome to the fast and furry-ious first GERONIMO STILTON 3 IN 1 graphic novel, featuring the first three GERONIMO STILTON graphic novels: "The Discovery of America," "The Secret of the Sphinx," and "The Coliseum Con," from Papercutz—those mousey-types dedicated to publishing great graphic novels for all ages. Oh, and I'm *Salicrup*, *Jim Salicrup*, the Editor-in-Chief and Fellow Time-Traveler (albeit in just one direction), here to look back in time at the early days of the GERONIMO graphic novels...

Perhaps one of Geronimo Stilton's greatest adventures has been kept a tightly-guarded secret—until now! This is the true-life tale of a little time-traveling mouse who saved a struggling graphic novel publisher from oblivion. Terry Nantier, publisher, and I started Papercutz in 2005, and we were off to a great start with a couple of graphic novel series, NANCY DREW and THE HARDY BOYS, that were flying off bookstore shelves. Things continued to do well for Papercutz the following years, but then 2008 came along. Historians have named the financial collapse that struck the entire world then as The Great Recession. When first signs of trouble appeared, the President of the United States of America warned citizens not to panic. So everyone panicked.

In the world of book publishing, books are sent by the publisher's distributor to bookstores and other booksellers to be offered for sale to the public. When books are sold, the money goes to pay the bookseller, the distributor, and the publisher. The publisher pays everyone who put the book together—the writers, artists, letterers, colorists, editors, printers, and everyone else involved in the book's production. But when a book doesn't sell, the bookseller can return it to the publisher, at the publisher's expense. In order to be a successful publisher, the number of books sold has to be far greater than the number of books that are returned. In 2008, the start of The Great Recession, booksellers panicked and we were getting almost all of our books back. Things didn't look too good for Papercutz.

Fortunately publisher Terry Nantier had previously made a deal for Papercutz to publish a new series of graphic novels, set to debut during the second half of 2008. That new series was... GERONIMO STILTON. Based on the advance orders, Macmillan, our wonderful distributor, was receiving, they were convinced that Papercutz still had a bright future ahead of us despite the then-current sad state of economic affairs. Encouraged by those advance orders for GERONIMO STILTON, our distributor made it possible for Papercutz to not only survive, but to actually thrive—2008 became our most successful year up to that point.

As the years pass, we'll never forget how much we owe GERONIMO STILTON and you! After all, it was your support and the support of thousands of GERONIMO STILTON fans, who during some of the worst recent economic times still kept getting GERONIMO STILTON graphic novels. So whether you were there back in 2008 or just now discovering GERONIMO STILTON graphic novels, we thank you for your support!

We hope you enjoyed GERONIMO STILTON 3 IN 1 #1, and that you'll be back for #2 which features the next three graphic novels: "Following the Trail of Marco Polo," "The Great Ice Age," and "Who Stole the Mona Lisa?"

See you in the future,

Oh, here's a little further info on our great mouse detective:

I'M HERCULE POIRAT, AND I'VE BEEN A FRIEND OF GERONIMO SINCE PRESCHOOL. I'M A CLEVER DETECTIVE AND RUN THE SQUEAK AGENCY. I LOVE TO PLAY TRICKS ON GERONIMO AND I'M A BANANA-MANIAC.

STAY IN TOUCH!

EMAIL: salicrup@papercutz.com
WEB: papercutz.com
TWITTER: @papercutzgn
INSTAGRAM: @papercutzgn
FACEBOOK: PAPERCUTZGRAPHICNOVELS
FAN MAIL: Papercutz, 160 Broadway, Suite 700, East Wing, New York, NY 10038

Thea Stilton

GRAPHIC NOVELS AVAILABLE FROM PAPERCUTZ

...ALSO AVAILABLE WHEREVER E-BOOKS ARE SOLD!

#1
"The Secret
of Whale Island"

#2
"Revenge of
the Lizard Club"

#3
"The Treasure of
the Viking Ship"

#4
"Catching the
Giant Wave"

#5
"The Secret of the
Waterfall in the Woods"

#6
"The Thea Sisters and
the Myster at Sea"

#7
"A Song for the
Thea Sisters"

papercutz.com